THE MATRON

DAWN GARISCH

THE MATRON

MYRMIDON

Myrmidon Books Ltd
Rotterdam House
116 Quayside
Newcastle upon Tyne
NE1 3DY

www.myrmidonbooks.com

Published by Myrmidon 2011

First Published as *Trespass* by Kwela Books, an imprint of NB Publishers,
40 Heerengracht, Cape Town, South Africa in 2009

A catalogue record for this book is available from the British Library.

ISBN 978-1-905802-61-6

Set in Garamond by Nazli Jacobs

Printed and bound in Great Britain by Martins the Printers

1 3 5 7 9 10 8 6 4 2

To those who went before

CAPE TOWN, UNION OF SOUTH AFRICA

1955

The matron's room is conveniently situated next to the sick bay. Mr Paine, the assistant housemaster who showed me around the school this afternoon, had opened the door, and a nauseating combination of sweet perfume, smoke and death emanated, catching at my chest. Mr Paine told me with a shake of his angular head that my predecessor had died suddenly, soon after watching a closely contested rugby match on the main field. He informed me with an air almost of reverence that she had followed the game keenly.

It would not be wise, I'd thought, to confess that I find rugby puzzling.

Entering my new bedroom, I was relieved to see my suitcase, which had earlier been whisked away from my taxi by the garden boy, lying across the chair. I'd had no reason to believe it was not in safe hands; my relief was entirely due to encountering a pocket of familiarity in a terrifyingly strange landscape. The brown and battered holdall, which

had belonged ...y father ...hose work took him all over Africa, was
waiting patie... ...or me. ...r Paine stood fidgeting at the door, closely
examining ...rchitra... ...e as I took in my new abode. That suits me.
I don't war... ...is pry... ...g eyes inside.
I will ...e to w... ...n the yellow paisley curtains and the bed covers
and ge...omeor... to help me carry the carpet downstairs for a good
biatig. It can... ...be too difficult to expurgate death, surely. Yet it took
two deaths to bring me here – two! How long Lord, till You send

death for me?

It has not escaped my attention that Mummy's passing away and
my changed circumstances have arrived soon after the time of the year
that we honour Your crucifixion, Lord. How much more difficult
were Your trials on this earth! Mine are nothing in comparison, so I
will stop complaining.

On reflection, it seems a bit harsh to remove immediately all signs
of the previous matron, poor thing.

Mr Paine could not contain himself any longer and announced
that he was required elsewhere, saying I should present myself at six-
twenty sharp at the north entrance of the dining hall where he would
introduce me to the other housemasters, Mr Talbot and Mr Leighton,
before dinner. I was relieved to see him stalk off on his thin legs; at
the same time, I became aware of a further constriction in my chest
at being abandoned to my fate. Mercifully, I have my asthma pump
for such circumstances, and this journal for comfort, and, of course,
You, God.

The room is tiny and painted with the same nauseating enamel
green as the sick bay. I note that there is no bookcase, which will have

to be remedied shortly, as my books will arrive on Wednesday. There is a bedside table and cupboard containing a few wire hangers that jangled forlornly as I hung up my coat, and a small table at which I am now seated with a rather grimy kettle on top. I have no need of further kitchen paraphernalia, Mr Paine told me as we walked past the dining hall earlier; I am expected to take my meals with the boys as part of my duties.

Once he had gone, I tried out the mattress, which sighed into the shape of the previous owner, exhaling more smoke to catch at my throat. I fear it will also bring nightmares and backache.

There is a consolation, though. From here, where I am sitting, I can see a goodly slice of my beloved mountain framed by the sash window. It is saturated today with the blue and lilac hues of early winter, with clouds curdled round the peak. This view will be an endless source of inspiration if I can find space in this small room for my paints. The lack of space is aggravated by there being two doors to this room, one that leads into the sick bay, and one into the corridor. I do not like this arrangement; it makes me feel as though I could be attacked simultaneously from two sides. I will ask permission to keep one of them locked.

Below the window, I can hear the incessant tumult of young male voices. This is my new and only home.

Recently, my eyes simply won't stop leaking.

⌖

It is with much trepidation that I begin this new life, and with it, this journal. I have not attempted such a record for decades, not since

I was a girl. Yet I find myself alone at this table with a pen in my hand and an exercise book in front of me, hoping that these scribblings can help me. This, and also my watercolours, albeit in different ways.

I am the kind of person life happens to. It might appear that I chose to come here, but it wasn't so. Mummy died, leaving me unexpectedly with no roof over my head because of an unfortunate debt of which I had no prior knowledge. Phoebe came down for the funeral, and happened upon an advert for this position that had miraculously become available. I am fated. God plants my every step.

The irony is that Mummy could not abide the rich, and warned against their pernicious company, yet because of her death I have arrived, hat in hand, at their doorstep. I will, however, take due precautions. Mummy was right in that money is a potential corrupter, particularly in combination with idleness. She need not fear, however, as in this position on my current salary, I will not be susceptible to the vices of the wealthy!

I have a carbon copy of my letter of application, stuck into the back of this journal. Phoebe looked it over before I sent it. She says I have a good handwriting, but I think the loops come out too childishly.

> Dear Mr Talbot,
> I would like to apply for your advertised position of Matron. I do not have experience directly in the field, but I was a student nurse for a few months after my schooling. Unfortunately, I had to leave before obtaining my diploma

as my mother was ill. Thereafter I worked in Mr Lawson's pharmacy situated in the Main Road for many years; thus I have a knowledge of routine medicines. An aspect of my employment was to attend to people who needed their dressings changed or their blood pressure taken. I have a good manner with people. Mr Lawson's kind reference is enclosed.

My hobbies are reading and walking. I am in good health, although occasionally troubled by minor episodes of asthma. I am a practising Anglican; Father Evans's reference is also appended.

I hope very much that you will grant me an interview. It would be an honour to be associated with your prestigious school.

Yours faithfully,

Phyllis Wilds

⌒

Dressed appropriately for the occasion, I hoped, in my newest frock (though no garment can compensate for frumpishness), I started out for the dining hall somewhat early, worried both about being late and not knowing in which direction north lies. On the way there, passing what I remembered as the staffroom on my tour with Mr Paine, I saw the light on inside. Through the door, which stood ajar, I could see Mr Paine, drink in hand, half listening to another, more animated gentleman with a rim of reddish hair around a shiny pate. I also caught a glimpse of another in the room, but I did not want to tarry for fear of being thought eavesdropping. As I continued towards the dining hall, sudden doubt caused panic to clutch at my chest. I was faced with the dilemma of whether to return to my room for my pump, thus risking being late for dinner, or to press on, so risking a full asthma attack in public view. Thus my thoughts ambush me, for I tend to think too slowly.

I could not properly recall Mr Paine's instruction – whether I should in fact be meeting the other housemasters before dinner in the staff-room north of the dining hall. The latter seemed to be the case, for that indeed is where they were. Time was marching on; it was apparent I would not have the chance to return to my room. I went back to the staffroom and, hesitating, I stood in the rectangle of light falling through the door, my heart racing. I had never been into a staffroom before; it had been strictly forbidden to enter it at the school I'd attended as a girl.

Reminding myself I was now a member of staff and no longer that little girl, and that all would be well, God willing, I entered to meet my colleagues. I retain a distinct image of the next few moments; it is fixed into my mind like a photograph in an album. Would that I could burn it to ash as I had those holiday snaps I'd found while clearing out Mummy's house. As I entered, my eyes sought out Mr Paine as my link with this new life. His gaze locked onto my face, and I saw his eyes widen with what I can only describe as shock, his mouth opening, about to shout out a warning. I found myself suspended in frozen time, anxiously awaiting clarification as to my error. All conversation stopped, as though a flipped switch had silenced a radio. My mind was imprinted with the image of the three besuited men, drinks in hand, staring at me in various permutations of anger and surprise.

I mumbled my apologies and fled.

                          ∽

It is a pathetic conceit to imagine that the act of destroying a photograph achieves anything substantial or consequential. The function of a photograph, it seems to me, is to point towards some inner constellation of thoughts, images, feelings and events. It provides a reminder of something that resides entirely within the mind's eye. Those holiday photographs, where Alan and I and Phoebe squint out of dead black-and-white time at a viewer situated in the present, do not transport me back to the exact moment each photograph was taken: where we are posed within the family setting, at the lunch table, or on the stoep, or trying to overturn the hammock with one of us in it; even those shots of us in the canoe or catching crabs do not remind me of the scald of sun on my back, or the salt sting of the wind. They point entirely to my shame and loss, those troublesome twins that live at my side, whether there be photographs or not.

Through the window Devil's Peak is sombre and brooding today, its large bulk leaning over me.

Over the years, I have often wondered what became of Alan.

                          ∽

I will never forget last night. I retired early after taking prep for the standard sevens, dispensing a few medicines and settling the junior dormitory entrusted to my care. I lay down on the lumpy mattress, confused and tearful. At table, no mention had been made of my blunder. The housemaster, Mr Paine, passed me the rice, but no one passed the gravy, and I was too frightened to ask for it, so went without. Mr Leighton, with the sparse red hair, spoke at length about the condition of the rugby field, and Mrs Talbot, from behind a thick layer of face powder, inquired in an idiot voice whether I had ever travelled outside the Cape. I mumbled a reply, for I am ashamed to say I have not even ventured as far as the sea since I was a girl. The sight of the sea holds certain memories I would rather not visit. Mrs Talbot then told me about her recent travels overseas with Mr Talbot, to Venice and Greece. Such extravagance in post-war times smacks of an inheritance; I was about to in-quire politely about her family when Mr Talbot glared at me and rang the bell for pudding.

I am a disgrace, and I do not know why, unless it is that women are not permitted in the staffroom. Indeed, Mrs Talbot had not been there.

For a while I lay in the darkness and scolded myself for making a mess of things on my first day, and also for my pathetic tendency to cry. I had left the curtains open, for I was having difficulty breath-ing, despite my pump. The night sky through a window has always appeared an escape, of sorts, ever since I'd brought disgrace upon my family. I feel Mummy still sitting heavily on my chest, pinning me down. Not a bad thing, really; I have always been a dreamer, and need to be disciplined and reminded of the task before me.

What I then heard as I lay in my room shocked me upright. A low roar sounded out, then another. I felt the vibration as though in my bones.

I thought I was going mad. Mad girl, Mummy used to say. Too much imagination for your own good.

But after a few more of the same, I was convinced. I realised that the sound could only be coming from the zoo, situated some miles away on the side of Devil's Peak. My suspicion was confirmed today at breakfast by Mrs Talbot. The night had been very still, and the majestic voice of the trapped beast travelled across the suburbs, which only served to increase my sadness. I wished to comfort him, to let the poor creature know he is not alone.

Lord, I do not mean to be disrespectful, but I am truly shaken by Your miraculous and prompt answer to my prayer! How am I to understand this? I know that Your invisible hand is in everything, but it was quite a shock to open the newspaper in the common room yesterday and to see Alan dressed in full academic gown and receiving an award. It was not an article I would ordinarily have read, but I noticed his face in passing, and it struck me, literally, like a fist to the chest: this is Alan! Of course, he is much changed, balding, but with the same unmistakable broad brow and shy smile. I checked, of course, and the caption confirmed that this was indeed Alan Harris – now a Professor of Zoology at the University of Cape Town. It appears that he has held this position for some time. I am so grateful that he survived the war.

I was so overcome that I tucked the newspaper under my cardigan and brought it to my room in order to cut the article out.

I have sat with him some hours again today. He is looking at and leaning slightly towards the photographer, or audience, as though about to pass comment, and the view of his face affords the tiniest glimpse of his tongue between his parted lips. I don't quite know why that should upset me so, but it does, with a kind of wrenching of the heart. His shirt collar above his gown is neat and well ironed, and his fingernails neatly manicured. The cuff link that is visible is engraved – presumably with his initials, presumably a gift. A gift from someone who loves him. He is still a very handsome man, to my mind, a man you'd want to meet should you spot him on the other side of a crowded room. The caption reveals that he is being honoured for his discoveries concerning the nervous system of frogs, for helping us to understand how it – and, by implication, our own – functions.

All those years ago, after a night flung about and torn by a violent storm, we were up early. After breakfast, we went down to the beach for a walk. It was a mess, strewn with clumps and stems of kelp; also with the small corpses of dozens of baby seals. Uncle Jack said it was because they were not strong enough to withstand the waves. I remember Alan's expression as he picked one up and examined its dead little dog face: intent, intense, full of a deep curiosity. I turned away, and ran ahead down the beach. I searched and searched, trying to find even one that was alive enough to put back into the sea.

Alan brought one of the carcasses home, wanting to dissect it, but his mother, thank the Lord, put her foot down and made him take it back to the beach. It amazes me – even then, he knew exactly what he wanted out of life. I am pleased he went ahead and achieved it.

Whereas I, on the other hand, am distressed to discover that the only thing I have ever really wanted is Alan.

Initially I did not notice that the view of Devil's Peak from my window includes the university, elevated as it is above the suburbs on the flank of the mountain. To think, all this time Alan has been living and working in Cape Town and I didn't know it! The Greek columns and ivy-covered buildings are clearly visible from here. They are within walking distance of this school; in fact, Mr Lawson's pharmacy is even closer. Might Alan have popped in one day for a bottle of antacid or some such thing during the time I spent as pharmacy assistant? Would I have recognised him? Of course – as I have now. Throughout those long summer holidays, my eyes never once left his face.

You have given me a sign, Lord, but what does it mean? You do not intend me to contact him, surely! Or do You? Now that You have taken Mummy from me, why have You conspired to show me Alan? He is surely living a full and extraordinary life, complete with a wife and children.

Does he harbour any curiosity about what happened to me, washed up by the terrible storm of my own life? Does he ever wonder what happened to little Kitty?

Perhaps he was never told. Or perhaps some people find it easier than others to put their past behind them and to start again. That is all. Some people remember, and some forget.

Forgive me for pointing this out, but this is bad timing, Lord. You do not take into account that I have just lost my mother and my home. I see now that this photograph You have placed in front of me is not an encouragement, but a punishment.

I must stop all these thoughts immediately, for they bring only misery. I will therefore crumple up his photograph and throw it in the wastepaper basket. This information is merely a minor setback. I have plenty of tasks to which I must apply myself, rather than dwelling on the past.

I wonder what it is like to cut open a frog, to pierce its skin with a lancet. I wonder what it is like to be a Professor of Zoology.

My first patient has arrived! Please, God, don't let me kill him. Brian Selby, a standard eight pupil, was sent to the sick bay by Mr Leighton with a fever and an infection that has gone to his chest. He is taller than I, which presented the first difficulty, but once he was prostrate and tucked up in bed, I was able to summon the maternal cheer I imagine is expected of me. I took his temperature and gave him two aspirin and some cough medicine and wiped his brow. At lunch time, I encouraged him to take a little broth, and eventually managed to suggest that he cough into the crook of his elbow so as not to spread his germs. One would have expected his mother to have taught him the basics, by his age!

Anyway, I am pleased to report that he generally listens to me, although he is a taciturn type. Perhaps I will be good at this job. Or good enough, at least.

Perhaps I can even go as far as to hope that I have found a real vocation.

I must say, this is not what I expected. It seems I am the only woman resident in this boarding house, one among three similar houses. Oh, there is the housekeeper, Mrs Williams, a triangular figure who glowers behind imposing spectacles topped by caterpillar eyebrows, and who keeps to herself. She is in charge of the kitchen and the cleaning staff, rules with a rod of iron, and oversees the making of wonderful soup. One of her girls who cleans the sick bay is banging a broom about under the beds as I write, to my irritation.

It is lonely without Ursula, who also doesn't drive but promises to catch a train to come and visit on a weekend.

This morning as I was taking in the vista of the mountain from my window, which also looks onto the grounds in front of the hall, I saw two women in a throng of scholars and teachers hurrying past on their way to the classrooms. I hoped that some women might perhaps be employed as teachers, or in the other boarding houses. This was later confirmed at chapel. From where I sat in the apse, I could make out five other womanly faces floating in a masculine sea: one about my age, only heavier, in a light floral dress; another rather thin and shrivelled one; one with a flounce of auburn hair; and a smart young thing dressed in red and black, with an unfortunate combination of nose and mouth suggesting an exclamation mark. Another sat near the back, so I could not make out her features very well apart from her grey hair and spectacles.

The standard seven boys in the pews around me squirmed and jigged during chapel, natural enough at their age, but I am expected to make them sit up straight and be still.

To tell the truth, I am a little afraid of them. I know nothing of boys as I have no brothers and attended a school for girls. Indeed, I would classify my present circumstances as a ghastly mistake if I did not believe that the Lord has brought me here for a purpose.

Father Nichols's sermon was about the nature of service, a subject close to my heart. He read the parable of the faithful servant: "Be dressed for action and have your lamps lit; be like those who are waiting for their master to return from the wedding banquet, so that ye may open the door for him as soon as he comes and knocks."

He impressed upon the boys that, just as Jesus's whole life had been one of service, so should theirs. Service to country, school, parents, teachers, and to God. He told them they were fortunate to be living in a time of peace and prosperity, and they should remember that this is a consequence of their parents' and grandparents' willingness to serve in two wars against Germany despite the personal cost to life and limb.

Then he read that wonderful passage: "From everyone to whom much has been given, much will be required; and from one to whom much has been entrusted, even more will be demanded."

Displayed on the wall beside us is a board inscribed with the names of past scholars who fell in the recent war, and across from us is the list of those who succumbed in the first. May it please You, Lord, not to allow these young ones around me to suffer the same fate. I know little of war, other than my father's stories about his service in Italy before he developed severe sepsis due to an ingrowing toenail, and was sent home – but I do pray we've seen the last of war.

Mummy, where are you? The world is so vast, so lonely. How is it that I have lost you, my home, my life?

I have been here for over two weeks already, two weeks into the rest of my time on this earth, to be lived in these circumstances.

Tonight someone else sleeps in my bedroom. Someone else wakes up each morning and lives my life. Someone else strokes and feeds my darling Blackie. I am cast out into a place of bones and shale and ash. I am nothing but drifting husk in a dry and incomprehensible landscape. I am nothing, worse than nothing – I am a nuisance. I know that is the reason Phoebe found me this job. Ursula has not visited me once, though she did phone.

Stop feeling sorry for yourself.

I might as well be dead.

⌒

I will make the best of things; I always do. We all have our duties, and some might appear easier than others. Phoebe has her doctor husband and her plush home in Sandton and her sons and a grand-child on the way, and I have this niche in the world. It can't be all that easy for her, juggling so much, and with Bryan always on call. It can't be easy at all. And Ursula has her music pupils and her dogs and stupid old George, who I very much doubt will marry her after all this time.

I am grateful. I have a roof over my head and food in my belly, and a small salary for sundries. My duties are not onerous, but the hours – another surprise – are long. I have one Sunday and one weekend off each month. If there are no patients in the sick bay, then the mornings, while the boys are in class, are mine to do with as I please. But there are about a hundred boys in this boarding house, and looking at the register, it is a rare occurrence for the sick bay to be empty. The absence of patients the day I arrived was a singular coincidence.

My charges have no mother to care for them here, and it will be my duty to provide them with a feminine touch in this male domain. They are the children I never had, the young men I never had the opportunity to love. In other ways, God has prepared me well – first awakening the maternal response so long ago, then giving me a mother that needed care.

I will not disappoint Him.

⌒

The gardens here, I must say, are a marvel and a comfort of sorts. This morning I decided to step out for some fresh air. A pair of sun-birds were flitting about in a pelargonium bush as though the world belonged to them, and a large bird of prey winged past, too high for me to identify.

I have found an ideal spot on a bench under the jacaranda – it is quiet but for the occasional intrusion of a schoolmaster's voice from the nearest classroom. I cannot imagine standing up and holding forth before a room full of boys, but then God in His wisdom did not make me a teacher. It must be a wonderful vocation to be able to open young men's minds with the tool of education. These fortunate boys are being prepared to reconstruct from the rubble of war what is best in the world. Many of them will graduate from this school and move on to the university. Some of them will be lucky enough to have Professor Harris as a lecturer. I am certain he is an inspiring mentor.

I sit with a book open beside me, brought to gather up my wayward mind should it wander off down some shadowy alleyway in search of mischief. My journal is open on my lap. If I tilt my head upwards I can see the intricate network of the branches of this beautiful tree. Each branch arrives at a fork. Each fork is a choice, offering different and subsidiary paths. It seems that I have always chosen the wrong one. So here I am, close to the ground, secreted away, while Alan has reached the apex.

You have made your bed, Phyllis, so now you can damn well lie in it.

I must remember: they also serve who only stand and wait.

What a joy I have discovered here! The library is a treasure house! All my old favourites, as well as authors I have never come across before. Mr Richardson, the head librarian, I find intimidating, but I do like his part-time assistant, Miss Judy van Breda. She has introduced me to a few contemporary women authors from her personal book collection, women of much integrity and writing skill, although I must admit that some of the notions put forward in the book by Katharine Butler Hathaway rather shocked me.

How I wish I could write; I wish I could confer as much pleasure on others as these women do.

I am at present rereading *Persuasion* from my own bookshelf, a book that troubled me deeply on my first reading of it. Miss Austen has a most disturbing way of getting to the heart of the matter. I am a Mary, but with no Colonel in sight to save me, other than my God. The flesh-and-blood man I turned away seventeen and a half years ago has never returned. Dear Hugo. But it could not be helped. I couldn't disappoint my parents yet again.

Just before leaving for the airport after Mummy's funeral, Phoebe told me that she had seen Hugo at a fiftieth birthday party in Johannesburg. She said he was doing quite nicely, working as a sub-editor for the *Rand Daily Mail*, with a lovely wife and two daughters. It seems that my sacrifice has made several people happy.

I carry knives in my heart. One of them is for Phoebe.

⌒

I shouldn't write in pen. I'd then be able to erase those terrible words, but to what end? God can read my mind as clearly as any text. If it is true that I carry knives in my heart, I might as well confess and seek absolution.

The irony is that the knives I carry for others keep cutting me, so that I am raw and bleeding. That is the real reason Jesus instructed us to forgive those that trespass against us. An attitude of revenge merely hurts oneself, keeping the old wounds open. Yet forgiveness does not arrive just because one wills it. I would have done better living in the time of Moses. An eye for an eye. A plague on my enemies!

These are blasphemous thoughts; I dig myself in deeper. Lord, forgive me.

Stupid, stubborn girl. Mummy was right. She said I was sullen, and wayward. She said it for years from her bed, which had become the centre of my existence; her bells and demands and complaints were the tethers that bound me to her. Also the fetter of that terrible error I would never be able to undo – the shame I brought on them all.

I am not complaining. It was fortunate I was in a position to care for her during the years Father was so frequently away on business. Yet I cannot ignore the feeling that Phoebe could have done more. She'd managed to escape the curse I'd cast on the family and married a man who I'm sure doesn't know to this day what I did. She followed Bryan to Johannesburg. Which she had to do, of course, what with him opening a surgery there. And then the children came, one after another. So she hardly ever found the time to get away, to come down and see her own mother. Or to bring her sons to see their grandmother and aunt.

It's a disgrace, and I can't pretend to understand it. I hope it happens to her some day – that her own flesh and blood avoids her. I hope that Pete and Frank and Robert abandon their mother in her sickness and old age.

Wicked girl.

I want to kill her. It's not something I'd ever admit to, but I want to push her down a flight of stairs.

⌒

At last I have met the matrons of the other houses – two of the women I'd first seen in chapel: a Mrs Calitz, who, it seems, has taken on the shape and smell of the cigarettes she incessantly smokes, and a Mrs Jones, who is rotund and off-puttingly hearty. Tweedledum and Tweedledee, my father would have called them. They do not like each other much, and have taken it in turns to warn me about the other.

"Two-faced bitch," Mrs Calitz spat.

"A real tattle-tale," Mrs Jones warbled.

Both have been married; Mrs Calitz has been divorced for many years now, and Mrs Jones is a widow. All three of us are here without other means of support.

I find I have very little to say to either of them. The other women I'd noticed are teachers, and I am unlikely to come into much contact with them.

⌇

What is it about names? I was aware of the titter that ran around the dining hall that first dinner. After we'd thanked the Lord for the provisions brought before us, the boys standing restless and hungry at their places, followed by the clamour of scraping chairs echoing in the high room as they seated themselves, Mr Talbot introduced me as the new matron.

"Matron Wilds," he said, "has been kind enough to join us at short notice."

Some boys glanced at each other, others suppressed a grin. I knew what they were on about. At school I was teased by my peers, and warned by the teachers not to live up to my last name. Names are an atrocious joke of birth and heritage, for I am plain, with a demure manner, yet one salacious glance from a tall, muscled boy at the head of the nearest table made me feel tarnished.

Occasionally I overhear the boys in the corridor, or outside my window, or chatting in the sick bay, and have discovered that most of the staff have nicknames. Poor Mrs Williams is "William" or "Billy", Mr Paine is predictably "The Pain", Mr Leighton is "Peachbum" – I have no idea why – and Mr Talbot is "Tailbottom". It is a mystery to me why males seem fixated on the behind as a source of hilarity.

The reflection in the mirror attached to the inside of my cupboard door stares coldly back at me. I am painfully aware that I have never been an oil painting, but lately I am shocked to discover how my features have disintegrated.

I shudder to think what the boys call me.

Every life has its routines, and I am pleased that I am at last settling into this one. On Monday and Thursday afternoons I witness a spectacle from my window. Rows of boys line up in uniform to go through a drill they call cadets. It looks like what I imagine the army to be, only these are small boys. Then I have to remind myself that boys of fifteen, sixteen years of age died in the war. This drill reminds me that we cannot take peace for granted.

Mr Paine takes the boys for cadets. Watching, unseen, from my room, I see how he is transformed by his task. It confers on him the bearing of a colonel. The boys appear to respond to this, and execute their movements in a choreography surprisingly pleasing to the eye.

I hear the rifle practice too, which takes place in the rifle range beyond the cricket oval; I am terrified of guns, and so will not venture there.

Thank God I am a woman, and am not required to participate in these strange but necessary functions. Yet I could have done more. I could have signed up to help in the war effort. But Mummy needed me at home, and I was terrified that with my smattering of nursing experience, I might end up somewhere having to deal with bones sticking out of bodies. That is something I could never do. Please, God, anything but bones sticking out.

⌒

Lord, dare I say it – You have a terrible sense of humour. I cannot believe that my life is still measured and interrupted by bells, despite my changed circumstances! Yes, I know full well there is a difference, but it is not, in essence, an improvement. Bells rule everything here, loudly demanding attention and punctuality at regular intervals during the day, pulling me away from my watercolours, or the sick bay; even from a book or reverie. Bells shrill, calling the boys to rise, to study, to meals, to school, to extramurals, to study again, to more meals, to shower and to bed, all responding to the timely right index finger of Mr Leighton, the assistant housemaster. Ringing the bell is amongst the duties he is required to perform in return for board and lodging. He is, in addition, a mathematics master of the lower grades. I have seen the boys mock him behind his back, for he is portly, with failing reddish hair and a mottled skin, and he has unfortunate mannerisms, frequently clearing his throat and wrinkling his nose, no doubt a consequence of allergies. He is the kind of person I imagine has been bullied all his life, and my heart would go out to him, only he is curt towards me, and largely ignores me at the dinner table.

Mr Leighton seems to live a lonely life, not unlike mine, tethered to institutionalised living by some private circumstance. What would bring a man in his midlife to live alone in an establishment such as this? Mr Talbot has his wife, and a house in the grounds, and therefore some semblance of normality to return to at the end of the day, whereas Mr Leighton, Mr Paine and I live at only a slight remove from the constricted life of the boarders in our little rooms reserved for staff. Mr Leighton does, I assume, leave the grounds from time to time, but only once have I seen him off the premises. As I entered the post office on the main road last week, a large man was exiting, and stood aside to let me pass. I saw at once that it was Mr Leighton, but he pretended not to know me, even when I thanked him by name.

There goes another bell; it is astonishing how that sudden ring causes a lurch of alarm within me. I forget momentarily where I am, thinking it is Mummy's little brass tea bell and I leap to my feet to see to her. But she is gone, gone, poor thing, and my eyes fill with tears. I must remember, as Father Evans would have me do, that she has now been released from her sickbed, and resides by the side of the Lord. He said I was an exceptionally good daughter, and that her passing on was a release for me too, in that I could now lead a more normal life. If only he had known, he would not have said such kind things, yet I could never bring myself to confess my childhood crime to him. It is perhaps divine justice that I was not released to a normal life after all – a life like Phoebe's – but to this, instead.

I must dry my eyes, and be brave. That bell beckons me to lunch, where I must sit and be ignored by Mr Leighton, and passed over by

Mrs Talbot, and suffer Mr Paine's embarrassment, and be patronised by Mr Talbot himself.

I dare not be late.

⌒

I was taken unawares today while immersed in my first attempt to paint the mountain. I almost jumped out of my skin when behind me I heard someone say what a pretty picture it was. I am quite certain I had closed the door before taking up a brush, yet I swung round to find the coloured cleaner, Grace, standing in the doorway to the sick bay, holding an armful of laundry. Pretty! What would she know of pretty, with her flat nose and that wiry hair sticking out from under her headscarf!

I told her that she was not to intrude into my private room. I will clean it myself, as I have always done. Mummy would never tolerate the extravagance of a maid, and I agreed with her, even though it made my duties more onerous. I know I should be grateful, as I don't pay Grace for her services, but I don't want anyone ferreting around in my private life, confined as it is. Yet the look on her face as she retreated made me feel guilty, as though I was the one who had done wrong. My concentration was ruined, and I was unable to return to my painting.

Pretty. I ask you!

What had she seen?

I felt cross for the rest of the day.

⌒

Ursula arrived this morning. I was both pleased and annoyed to see her. It has been almost two months since Mummy's funeral. Surely she knows how much I need support in this difficult time? I cannot express my disappointment in case she disappears in a huff forever, so I smiled at her and hugged her, and gave her tea.

It being a Saturday I felt obliged to attend the rugby game, so we went down to the grounds and sat under the oaks and conversed while the drama of balls and mud and bull-like boys played out before us. I'd been looking forward to her visit to tell her about my new and strange circumstances – after all, I have been here for nearly a month. But George had let her down again last night when she'd had tickets to the theatre. I found it hard to conceal my irritation. Why Ursula cannot bring herself to tell him to go to blazes is beyond me. She must know by now he is not going to leave his horrid wife.

Father Evans said that if you bring a problem to the Lord once, He will listen. If you bring it twice, still He will listen. But if you bring the same problem three times, there is something you need to do about it for yourself. Ursula has been bringing the problem of George to me for fifteen years! I am obviously more long-suffering than the Lord.

She says I am lucky to be here, what with no cooking and laundry to do, and with this I must agree. The food is quite reasonable, better than what I managed to make at home. She did add, with that disparaging note that only Ursula can achieve, that I have put on weight and will have to be careful.

It is a comfort, food, and lately I have felt in need of comfort. Besides, who would I be keeping trim for? Ursula laughed when I said this, and encouraged me to keep my eye open, there must surely be a suitable father or schoolmaster around! Ursula likes to shock, and can be unpredictable at times, so my concern mounted as she started surveying the crowd that was watching the rugby, identifying men she thought might be worth the effort. I rather suspect she was on the lookout herself as revenge on poor George. Much to my alarm, she identified both Mr Talbot and Mr Paine as possibilities.

The real problem with Ursula, as I frequently remind her, is that she has not yet found the Lord.

Yesterday morning I was again attempting to translate into colour the light falling onto Devil's Peak. I couldn't achieve the deep hues required to show the depth of fold in the mountainside; instead it came out dead and flat. Also, I was trying to decide whether to include the university buildings, a skill that is probably beyond my capabilities. I have never before attempted to paint buildings, confining myself rather to landscapes. I laid my brush down, wanting to weep with frustration, when there was a knock at the door, and a scholar informed me that Mr McCullough needed attention in the sick bay.

As I entered, he turned from the basin where he was wiping his hands on a towel, leaving an annoying red stain on it. He limped across to me, introducing himself as Mr Rory McCullough. He is a man somewhat younger than I, with a wayward cowlicked head of dark brown hair crowning a face set with the bluest eyes I have ever seen. At first I did not know whether it was his leg he'd come for or his hand, but then he thrust a bloody palm at me. He said he was the art master, and that he had been trying to put up shelving when the screwdriver slipped.

I noted alcohol on his breath. There was no mistaking it, and I felt myself stiffen at the thought: a master, drunk at school! Yet he did not seem drunk, but was instead charming. Indeed, I have been known to confuse these behaviours. Perhaps it was turpentine, I decided, giving him the benefit. He had a puncture wound on his palm, nothing that needed stitches in my opinion, but as I cleaned it, I suggested he return the following day to see Doctor Cudgel, who visits twice a week. There was a lot of red on his hand that was not blood, and he joked that he was going through his "red period". I almost exclaimed that I thought that only happened to women, but stopped myself in time.

Disgusting, the thoughts that spring to one's errant mind!

Mr McCullough explained that when he was in a fury, as he was at the time, rather than putting his fist through a window, he took his anger out on a canvas. Sensible, I thought, thinking also that the puncture wound belied him. What could have enraged him so? I felt afraid of this violent, friendly man who was telling me rather more than I should know. At the same time I was strangely interested in him, and inquired about his leg, whether it too needed attention.

He looked at me intently, as though surprised by something on my face, then, without answering my query, leaned further towards me. Alarmed, I started back, thinking he might kiss me, but he licked his thumb and wiped it across my cheek. Examining it, he exclaimed, "Watercolour!" and stared at me from under his brow as though I had committed a sin. I wished for him to leave so as to wash the shaming paint and his saliva off my face, suddenly embarrassed to be alone with a strange and unpredictable male. I stood up to indicate our encounter was over, or that I was duty-bound to leave – anything, anything but suffer this humiliation and confusion.

To my horror, instead of submitting to the dictates of polite convention, Mr McCullough raised his shirt and showed me his abdomen, which was grooved with long and ugly scars. "Shrapnel," he explained. "Buggered my leg, too." He lowered his shirt, and winked, I thought, at my distress. "Not much you can do about that now, is there?"

"I really must . . ."

"Don't worry, I'm off." At last he stood. "You can use the art room, if you'd like," he offered. "I might even rustle up some oils for you."

"I don't paint," I declared, which is not a lie. I dabble; I am a dabbler. No one could possibly confuse me with the real thing.

Again, that unnerving stare. A rude man, actually; one I do not wish to have dealings with.

"Thanks," he said, waving his bandaged hand at me. "And good luck here. I hope you can swim."

Now what could he possibly mean by that?

He lurched off down the corridor, his shirt hanging out for all who passed to see, leaving me red, red and raging.

⌒

It was a presumption to apply for this job. I am hopelessly under-qualified, and am afraid I might kill or maim someone through my abysmal ignorance.

Today I was summoned urgently to attend to a boy called Robinson who lay unconscious and bleeding from the nose after a collision during rugby practice. In my fright, I thought he might be dead; in the event he wasn't, and with the boys' expectant eyes on me crouching at his side, all I could think of doing was to take the scarf from around my neck and pinch it to his nose. The bone beneath his skin clicked horrifyingly between my fingers, the pain of which roused the boy, who moaned and tried to push my hand away. Fortunately, Doctor Cudgel arrived before I could do any further harm. I watched him shine a torch into the boy's eyes and press the back of his neck. He then told the boy to wiggle his toes, and asked some questions about where he was and what time of day it was. Satisfied, he led him off to the sick bay to plug his nose.

As a result, I am slightly more confident I'll know what to do should this happen again, only I am not at all sure what the good doctor was looking for in the poor boy's eyes.

The mountain is different again today. Every time I sit here, pen in hand, I pause to look out of the window at the magnificent rock that God has thrust from the ground, at the shifting shades and hues that the changing winter weather and light bring to bear on the mountain's timeless grace. This mountain is the one solid thing I can rely on, that is always there when I raise my eyes. It is my guardian, my touchstone, my anchor. It is the constant that has followed me to this new life. It is a manifestation of God on earth.

It is nine-thirty. I wonder what Alan is doing now, at work in those beautiful buildings of the university.

So near, yet so far.

I will try to paint her again today, despite there being only two hours between the tea-time and lunch-time bells; also, there are three youngsters with influenza needing medication and care in the sick bay. The view of the mountain from my bedroom window here is quite different to the view from the study at Mummy's home, and therefore more challenging, as though I have suddenly seen a different aspect of a person I have known for many years. Whereas before I looked towards Nursery Buttress, now my window faces Devil's Peak. Somewhere within the skirt of trees covering the mountain flank is my lion. I heard him again last night, when the wind dropped and all was quiet. You have set humans above the animals, Lord, and look what we have done with this responsibility. We have much we must atone for. I will honour him by suggesting a flick of golden flame amongst the trees – a hint of his escape.

Today a wad of cloud lies banked up over the city, releasing a wispy spill of mist over the mountain saddle towards the university. The contrast of mist with the solid bulk of mountain is perfect; it will be a challenge to transpose the image into paint.

I will start now, laying out newspaper on the floor, preparing the paper and setting out the paints and brushes. I am irritated to notice how a certain thought keeps occurring to me nowadays – Mr McCullough's invitation to use the art room, and also his offer of oils. I have used watercolour for years, there is absolutely no need for change. Besides, I can make do in my bedroom, although it is not ideal. To venture into the art room would expose myself and my muddled efforts. No one has witnessed this harmless pastime, not since Phoebe and her little joke years back that it looked as though the dog had relieved himself on the paper.

⌇

What am I to do? I find myself in situations here that no woman should have to face, and I do not know how to proceed. Two boys were clearly breaking house rules by being in the dormitory during lunch break, but I fear that their misdemeanour is far more serious than that. At first I thought they were fighting, as they were grappling, and grunting against each other.

Father help me, for they know not what they do. Stupid, stupid boys! This is how easily Satan has his way. They are young, and far from home; they both long for love and want to be men before their time. They do not understand yet that lust leads to undoing, to a turning to whosoever is at hand.

It is a sin, but I cannot possibly report it, neither to Mr Talbot, nor to Father Nichols. I do not even have the words for such a thing! Besides, I was so flustered I forgot to ask their names, and I am not sure I want to remember their faces.

Perhaps I was mistaken. They may have been engaging in a bit of horseplay, nothing more.

I will put it right out of my mind. If I in fact saw what I think I saw, it will most likely happen again, and I pray that You, Lord, will lead someone else to the scene of debauchery, someone more fit than I to intercede.

⌇

Mr McCullough has been pestering me again, asking what it is I paint, even asking me to show him. He came to the sick bay this morning to discuss some art history with Gregory Purvis, who was laid low with an infected spider bite on his leg, but soon enough Mr McCullough asked me for a cup of tea. I could not refuse him, even though I have to make it in my room. He hovered at the doorway while I put the kettle on, his eyes roving, then asked me where I keep my work. At first I did not know what he was talking about, for it is a mere pastime, a hobby. Luckily I had nothing out; it was all rolled away in the bottom of the cupboard, but eventually I had to admit that I paint the mountain, gesturing through the window at the magnificent peak. At this point he came right into my room, ostensibly to look through the window. What would Gregory and the other sick boy, Kenneth, think! The art teacher in the matron's bedroom! And I don't even know if there is a Mrs McCullough!

It was very awkward, but I managed to steer him out and into the procedure room, where, instead of taking a chair, he leaned against the examination couch so that he towered over my seated figure. This made me even more uncomfortable, as though I had let things slip, and had no control over the situation. He has chameleon eyes, Mr McCullough has, eyes that change from blue to green, and an engaging way of talking. And talk he does, this time about the new senate law. My good father used to say that one should leave politics to the politicians. I, for one, therefore know absolutely nothing about it. But to hear the art teacher talk about this law, one would think *him* a politician! On and on about the National Party government and what crooks they are. Thankfully the dinner bell saved me, and I was able to excuse myself, but even at table the conversation was full of it. I gathered from it all that the National Party wants to remove coloured voters from the roll, but they need a majority in the senate to do so. This they do not have, and so they are changing the constitution so that they can load the senate with National Party members, thereby achieving the majority they need.

This is indeed not fair, but what is one to do about it? There are all sorts of things in life that are unfair that one has to put up with. The world will always be full of sin because men do not heed the Word of God. But He has reassured us – when His Kingdom comes to earth all wrongs will be righted.

It is pointless getting all worked up about matters that are beyond one's control.

~

Roger Granger is the biggest boy I have ever come across, bigger than most men, which is why he is such a hero on the rugby field. He is a bulldozer, churning up everything in his wake on his way to score a goal. I know, because he is responsible for a good few of the injuries I see after rugby practice. Terrifying. And he is only in standard eight.

Today Adam Stanford was taken off the field on a stretcher with a knee swollen and flailing from a tackle by Roger. I saw it myself, for I am expected to attend games despite the doctor also being present.

I hurried over to assist Doctor Cudgel, praying that there would be no bones sticking out. I'd seen this once, as a schoolgirl, when one of the teachers broke her ankle in a gutter, and it has ruined me for life: the foot at an impossible angle, the splinters of bone poking through flesh. Dreadful. I feel sure I would faint again, and risk losing my job.

Why is it that schools and parents volunteer their children for this massacre? Have we not endured enough violence in war?

Poor Adam is off to hospital and the operating theatre. I doubt his knee will ever be the same again.

～

My quiet time this morning was disturbed by a terrible crash. In my fright, I stupidly thought that Mummy had fallen out of bed, but it was only Grace, who had knocked a rather attractive vase off the table in the sick bay. Shards and daisies were scattered all over the floor. I clucked my disapproval, for what good is a cleaner who is clumsy? I told her I had a good mind to send her off to Mrs Williams, and to see to the cleaning myself. One doesn't know with these people, what germs they might bring in from the places they live – TB and suchlike – and I would hate the few precious items I possess to go missing. Mummy's wedding ring, for example, that I took from her body before Phoebe could annex it. I wear it occasionally on my right hand. It is very plain, but beautiful in its simplicity, symbolic of the vow my parents made to each other.

There are certain things one wouldn't want to live without. There are things that are a reminder of what might have been.

Anyway, Grace dropped to her knees to help me clean up, but before long she had dissolved into tears, which made me feel guilty for speaking sharply to her. I tried to placate her, but she wouldn't stop weeping, so I got annoyed with her again, and told her to pull herself together. I will ask Mrs Williams to send me someone else, for I cannot abide a manipulator.

I dread prep. Every day I feel my anxiety rise as five o'clock approaches. The standard seven boys are seated at their desks, and I am at the teacher's, facing them. Before me is a room full of boys; although this is only their second year of high school, some are already becoming young men. A few are taller than I am, and their soft chins are hardening and sprouting facial hair. They are young and restless and foolish. I do not pretend to understand them, and they take advantage of my fright. I take a book to while away the time, and to keep my eyes averted.

About a week ago, I was sitting reading an early Dorothy Sayers, ignoring the murmur of voices, hoping they would stop of their own accord, when something stung my forehead, then dropped to the page. I examined it: a small, tight, damp ball of paper. Another struck my nose to the sound of stifled laughter. I brushed them off the book, and carried on reading, pretending nothing had happened, until the constant pelting and outright laughter could no longer be ignored. I raised my head to see a welter of boys hurriedly hiding their rulers and suppressing guffaws, bending their heads dramatically over their desks; from the back burst a loud snigger. I stood, leaning against the desk, appalled to feel my legs shaking underneath me with rage and fear, horrified to hear my quaking voice pipe out from between my lips. "Please stop it. Get on with your work."

But the rain of small chewed balls of paper, and the mutter, and the muffled laughter continues intermittently. I know how they see me: a useless old woman, a nuisance, good only for a laugh at her own expense. I am mortified, miserable, terrified. What if Mr Talbot discovered my incompetence!

I want to plead with them: I need this job; please, do not make me lose it.

⤿

What to do! I have confronted Grace, for it can only be she who has stolen from the dispensary cupboard. I am such a fool! It should always be locked, but I turned my back for fifteen minutes, distracted by the kettle almost boiling dry, and in that time a bottle of painkillers and one of cough mixture was removed. I cannot believe that the culprit was either James Winters or Ian Fairbrother, the two in the sick bay at present; they are not that kind of boy. Whereas Grace, when I asked her, looked guilty, I could see it in her eyes, but she denied it vehemently. Her lie jeopardises my employment, and I am already anxious about my tenure here. I would report her, but if my lapse is discovered, I might be thought unfit to carry the dispensary keys, which is one of my main duties.

There is no other way but to conceal Grace's theft by replacing the items myself, which I can ill afford. At the same time I will communicate with Mrs Williams that I do not want Grace to work in this area again.

Why don't these people understand the merits of honesty? This is exactly why Mummy wouldn't have them in the house.

I must remember to lock away the sherry in my cupboard.

⤿

I must stop this weeping. It cannot be good for one's tear ducts. Under my window earlier today I overheard the names they call me. My hateful name, Phyllis, they have twisted into Vullisblik, the Afrikaans for rubbish bin. And also Wild Phallus. I had to look up the meaning of the word.

They must surely know that this is my window. Either I am invisible, or they want me to know what they think of me. I am so embarrassed.

They have all seen through you. Stupid, ineffectual girl.

⌒

A letter from Phoebe! This is an uncommon event, and of course, she wants something of me. I have little to give; therefore letters from her are rare. This appeal, however, takes the cake. Our dear Phoebe has taken to politics! Imagine that, when she has a busy husband who needs her attention and a grandchild about to arrive. She tells me there is a petition being circulated by a group of women protesting against the proposed change to the constitution. She has enclosed some papers, asking me to help collect signatures. Suspecting that Phoebe was, as usual, exaggerating, I dipped into the newspaper in the common room, but saw this news reported there.

What good do they think a petition will do? Besides the pros and cons of the argument, when have men ever listened to women? Even from her sick bed, Mummy failed to make an impression on Father. I had the notion he had stopped listening to her years before. That terrible morning, when he was about to leave on a business trip to Northern Rhodesia. Mummy had had one of her attacks after a fight

I'd overheard, where she accused him of not loving her any more. She was struggling to breathe, and I called the doctor who said he was going to put her in hospital as a precaution. My father looked at me as though he couldn't wait to escape, and told me to deal with it, he had a train to catch. He looked as though he had already left for somewhere better, as though his life with us was hell. The brown holdall was waiting for him in the hallway. It never left his side all those years he travelled to Nyasaland, Southern and Northern Rhodesia, and Bechuanaland. Thinking of it now, that same holdall stored next to my cupboard contained the whole of his real life, a life that had absolutely nothing to do with his errant daughter and his invalid wife.

I do not like Phoebe's handwriting, the way it slopes backwards, also in a hurry to get away. What use, in the end, was her flight to Johannesburg? Here she is, still clutching at straws. Unlike Phoebe, I hold no illusions about saving the world. I cannot even save myself.

Lord, please stay with me tonight. These are blasphemous thoughts that have no doubt displeased You. My pump has become less effective since I moved here. It must be the damp, and my fright at being so alone. Mummy had me to care for her through her long nights of suffering. Who will care for me? I am afraid, and fear always goes to my chest. I am sick and tired of the malfunctioning bagpipe I have become. I dare not speak to Doctor Cudgel, for if he should speak to Mr Talbot about my condition, I might be deemed unfit for the position of matron.

I must simply sit it out, and put all unhelpful thoughts aside, and pray that my cough does not wake the three boys in the sick bay and thereby betray me. The light will eventually come, it always does, no matter how interminable the night might seem.

⌐

Now that I have all the time in the world, I have not been able to put pen or brush to paper. The darkness closed in again once the boys had gone home for the mid-year vacation. It is a contrariness of character that I now miss the uproar in the corridors that I recently thought would drive me mad.

For the past week, since the teachers have also gone on leave, I have spent most of my time in bed. The deep winter weather is appalling, but that is no excuse. I have books and my painting to occupy me, yet I have not been able to rouse myself, nor my spirit.

One would expect to become accustomed to being alone. One would also expect to accept after many years the loss of those one has loved, or tried to love. One wonders what the nervous system of the frog might reveal about these human failings.

Today is Sunday, and I am determined to go to church. Yet as I look out of the window, another squall hits, and I cannot face squelching through this deluge in order to catch a train to Father Evans's parish.

God help me. I am drowning.

⌐

I am my own worst enemy; I always was, and always will be, for now and evermore. This afternoon I took to my brushes with intent, but it was not long before I crumpled the paper (which I can ill afford to waste), and marched downstairs to calm myself in the fresh air.

Every now and then I do a circuit of the grounds for exercise or give myself a good talking to. At this time of the year the switchblade strelitzia blooms are out along the tennis court fence, piercing the air with colour, and a tumble of lilac bougainvillea adorns the north side of the hall. A bed of aloes hold their bold orange batons up to the sun and curl their spiky leaves that remind me of crayfish legs.

On either side of the boarding house entrance stand two huge hibiscus plants decked with blooms like flamboyant red skirts. The gardens here are splendid, with such a variety of plants that one would never be short of flowers at any time of the year. Various proteas and ericas are coming out, as well as some magnificent roses, and I await the treat of vivid azalea. I must congratulate the estate manager, Mr Jansen, for his foresight and attention. The sight of such abundance both soothes and saddens me, for who am I? A mere nothing, a piece of unworthy dirt in the face of God's perfect artistry. His hand is everywhere, in the crushed smell of pine needles, the flung gesture of a dark branch, the fine and hopeful sprig of bottlebrush. I cannot possibly emulate this in paint; to try to do so is a conceit.

I will take up knitting again; I was good at it once. It is a noble and womanly art that serves several functions, as opposed to painting, which serves no purpose at all except as a dismal copy of the Great Creation.

One dreadful winter several years ago, Father Evans asked for volunteers to knit for the poor, and I have always regretted not heeding the appeal. I will set about it now, and overcome my resistance. It is the devil that stays my hand, the devil that licks at my ear with his split tongue, reminding me. As a girl I tried to knit my way out of shame; now, at the mere touch of wool or the click of needles, I feel evil shadows lap at my ankle.

That baby I knitted for is grown now. I have always hoped her mother made use of the little frocks and booties. I hope she told her daughter that she arrived in her new home with a suitcase full of woollen garments and a crocheted blanket.

I pray every day that that little girl has forgiven me.

⟜

Goodness! Sherry is a weakness of mine, and the rascal has sniffed it out. I am not in my right mind, yet I must try to jot down aspects of this evening's encounter before I forget. Tomorrow I shall be mortified, but tonight the sky is full of stars, and even the moon smiles down on me.

I had Mr McCullough knocking on my door this afternoon. He is back from his holiday, full of his usual banter, but it was a diversion to see him. He had brought some doughnuts to have with coffee, and I felt so grateful to be remembered that I offered to help him prepare the art room for the boys' return tomorrow. I have never been into a proper art room before, and I was astonished by what some of the boys had achieved in the last term with a still life of pomegranates broken open next to a green wine bottle. Then Mr McCullough, who still insists I call him Rory, brought out a catalogue he had acquired of a European painter I have never heard of called Chaim Soutine. Looking at the prints of Soutine's large oils, I entered an extraordinary dream. His landscapes and portraits lured me over a vertiginous edge; for a terrible moment I felt like weeping. One portrait is of a young girl with a coarse and reddish face; she stares ignorantly and unashamedly out of the frame to her right. The shocking thing about her is that she is naked. While her face is that of a naïve child, she has a woman's body which, though somewhat homely, is one I imagine a man might desire. I want to protect her, get her dressed. I want to smack her across the face. She doesn't know who she is, or what she wants, or anything about the world.

I became aware that Mr McCullough, Rory, was staring at me staring at her, and rapidly turned the page, my face reddening. I felt as naked and stupid as the girl.

"He has something, don't you think?" he asked.

I looked at the next painting of houses that appeared somehow meshed at impossible angles on a hilltop with trees, and marvelled at the effects the artist achieved by the manner in which he applied his brush, and his use of disorienting perspectives. The scene was unreal, yet it captured something essential about the setting. I managed a nod as answer, but thought back to yesterday, and my vow to forgo all this. The truth is I am weak. No sooner have I planned a course of action than I do the opposite. There is a caged beast in me that will not leave me alone, that seeks escape.

One weak moment leads to another, and half an hour later I had a sherry in my hand, and was appraising an unfinished painting of Rory's that he'd produced from his office – if "painting" is the correct word to apply to such a work. It looked as though he had attacked the canvas with meaty reds run through with black and silver blue;

although the shapes were indistinct, the scene reminded me of an abattoir, or of war, where the membranes of the inner cage of ribs were exposed – some such carnage involving bloody carcasses and cold steel. He asked me what I felt about it. I froze in the spotlight of such a question as though struck by stage fright. I don't know what is good and what is not, or even what I like and do not like. Also, I do not wish to offend, so I replied that it was nice. Rory's snort underlined the inadequacy of my response, and the offence he had taken.

I slowly surfaced to hear Rory going on about painting as a means to expose an inner reality, and to understand desire. His argument both interested and frightened me. I ventured to say that investigating desire carried the risk of being swept away into danger. I gave examples ranging from alcohol – as I waved my glass of sherry about – to adultery. He retorted that too safe a life is no life at all, and one might as well join a nunnery (which did once occur to me, yet I dared not protest that it might well be a profitable kind of life).

Then, so as to "prove" his point, he showed me a book about Mr Picasso, whom I know is very famous, but I do not claim to understand his kind of art at all. In the book, Mr Picasso pronounces that where art is chaste, it is not art. He claims that art *must* be dangerous, and that it ought to be forbidden to ignorant innocents! Well, that must include me. I was upset by all this. Mr Picasso obviously does not know his Bible. Why, then, should his arguments have any sway at all? I wished to argue with Rory, who had clearly been influenced by such types, but I felt too upset to open my mouth, and merely sat and nodded as though I not only followed his argument, but agreed with it. To think, he teaches young innocents himself! One wonders whether the authorities are aware of all this.

Rory went on, arrogantly proclaiming that experimenting both in life and on canvas develops one's capacity.

For what? one might ask!

I noted that he filled his glass at least twice as often as he did mine.

He argued that painting an atom bomb explosion was not the actual dropping of one, yet it had the potential to change the world, or explode the way people think.

Again I wanted to argue with him. After all, he bears the real scars of war on his abdomen, a war that had in fact helped to change the world in a way no painting ever could, but I was afraid he might expose himself again, and I was worried I had perhaps lost the thread of the argument. The dinner bell alerted me to the time, which I was shocked to discover had slipped away. I was expected to dine with the housemasters, it being the evening before the boys returned, but I felt concerned that I was in no fit state to do so, with sherry on my breath and my thoughts a trifle muddled. Stepping into the corridor, I intercepted one of the kitchen girls and sent word that I was feeling off-colour, and would not be attending dinner tonight. In the art room, I prepared to make my excuses, only to find that Rory had topped up my glass again, and was teasing me about being a liar. I could feel myself getting upset, but when he began clowning around, saying that artists need to be both liars and truth-tellers at the same time, I softened. It must have been the old devil alcohol persuading me I was included in the definition of "artist". He then asked me what off-colour I thought I was, and I skittishly replied, "Blue", for I have been feeling a little low of late.

He then dug out a blank canvas, set it upon an easel and offered me the most extraordinary range of blue oils to play with. Play! That is the word he used, whereas I have always approached prepared paper with the utmost solemnity.

Of course, I refused, although the devil in me looked longingly at the rich indigo, cobalt, ultramarine. It is wrong for a teacher to tease or tempt a student above their station, and I wanted to tell him so. But instead – having been brought up not to waste – I finished the rest of the sherry and explained that I had to prepare for my duties, which even to my ears sounded somewhat false. He shrugged and smiled, and said I was welcome any time. He added: "It's a way out of here."

Now what would he mean by that?

⌒

For what purpose, Lord, do You conjure these nocturnal visions? You, the Creator of everything, who sent dreams to the prophets to enlighten and guide us, why do You send these to me?

This pen slips in my gloved hand. It seems I will never get warm.

It was very real. I can still feel the hard ridge of scar tissue at my fingertips. An abdomen marked with scars presented itself close to my face, like a painting. I found myself tracing the shape of the solid weals, trying to discern the underlying landscape or portrait. The ridges of tissue where his flesh had been cut open guided my inquiry. I could not see the man's face, but since the belly was covered with dark hair,

I wondered whether it might not be Alan's; only, he had been little more than a boy all those years ago when I'd first seen his appendix scar. It occurred to me that this might be Jesus – but I knew then that it must be the art teacher's abdomen; I traced and drew, first with my finger, then with a sharpened knitting needle. I watched, fascinated, as blood beaded through the abrasions and ran down into his groin. Instead of protecting himself, he allowed it. I am ashamed to say I desired him, as I imagine a man desires. I wanted to penetrate him, to lance open the dull membrane of scar and enter him.

I will never be able to look at Mr McCullough again after this, let alone speak to him, for I am afraid he will see traces of the dream in my face. It has been sent as a warning, one that verifies my concern that "playing" with the things one desires can only end badly.

I am a living example of this.

The lion has been silent these past nights. His roar has been drowned by the winter wind, or he has given up hope and lies quietly behind his fence in the dark.

⌐

The church clock has just struck two o'clock and I am awake and ill at ease. A new boy named Adrian Flower was brought into the sick bay yesterday with a bad bout of vomiting. He was so poorly that I almost called Doctor Cudgel, but the boy had no fever and soon afterwards he kept some thin soup down. I then decided there was no need to trouble the doctor and that Adrian could wait to see him on the doctor's usual visiting day.

Before retiring, I went to see how he was doing. He was alone, as

John Thompson-Jones was well enough by the afternoon to go back to his dormitory. Going over to say good night, I saw by the night light that the blankets were covering his face, so I assumed he was asleep. As I turned away, a sob tore from his body. I was at a loss as to what to do, so I leaned over and rubbed his shoulder. It frightens me that I must mother these burgeoning creatures who are in many ways so foreign. I asked him whether it was his stomach, and he nodded yes – relieved, it seemed, to be presented with a way to explain his tears. Privately, I thought it was probably due to homesickness; he had told me on admission that his parents live in Johannesburg.

It is very strange to me that parents bother to have children, only to send them away for strangers to bring up. While patting Adrian's shoulder, my thoughts wandered to my own dear child, sent away to strangers so long ago. I feared I might also begin to sob, but that would never do, and so I briskly fetched an antispasmodic from the dispensary, and encouraged him to drink it with a little warm water.

He took the syrup without a fuss, then thanked me with a look of such terror on his damp face, speckled with pimples and freckles, that it clutched at my heart. I sat down on the bed and started to talk to him to keep the dark at bay. I told him that I was also new at the school, and that I was sure he would get used to it, and soon make some friends. But as I talked, his pallor increased. Excusing himself, he suddenly stumbled out of bed and headed for the bathroom, doubled over his cramping abdomen, then passed a wet wind accompanied by a dreadful faecal smell. I tried to help him to the bathroom, but he stopped in the middle of the room with a bout of vomiting;

at the same time I saw a horrid brown slop slide out of his pyjama leg onto the floor.

There were times, in the last few months of Mummy's life, when I'd had to deal with incontinence. But this was far worse, as the boy was beside himself with pain and embarrassment. I led him to the bathroom and propped him, weak and unable to look at me for shame, on the toilet, then I ran a bath, telling him to strip and clean himself. I returned to the sick bay to clean up the mess, sick with worry. Though it was late, well after ten o'clock, I felt that the doctor should be notified. My instruction was to let the head of house know before phoning for medical assistance. This would mean leaving my charge and venturing out across the grounds to Mr Talbot's house. I fetched newspaper and a bucket and mop, considering my course of action, concerned that I should have acted sooner, and what the consequences of not doing so might be. As I wiped the floor, I noticed, in the vomit, pieces of a flat yellow substance that did not look like food. Once the floor was clean, I went to the bathroom and listened at the door, inquiring after the boy's health. He insisted he was all right, so I put out clean pyjamas and went to notify the housemaster.

Mr Talbot opened the door and peered out at me as I explained the situation.

"Adrian?" he puzzled.

"Adrian Flower," I added. "The new boy."

"Oh, Flower!" he nodded, then looked at me sternly. "We only use the surname here," he advised. "It will embarrass him to do otherwise."

Why on earth? I wanted to ask. Instead, I bit my tongue, wrapping my coat about me in the winter chill, wanting only to hurry back to the poor creature.

Mr Talbot said he would call Doctor Cudgel immediately, and that I should stay with the boy until he arrived.

Adrian was in bed again when I returned. I told him that the doctor was on his way. He turned to the wall, curling around his stomach. I tried again, telling him not to worry, it could happen to anyone, and that he would be all right.

I had to ask: "There were pieces of yellow in your vomit. What was that?"

"Nothing, ma'am," he said, then burst into tears.

Something was not right, but I hadn't the experience to know what it might be. I took the boy into my arms and asked, "What is it? What?"

"I'm so scared," he said, not resisting my embrace.

"Why?" I asked. "I won't tell," I promised.

"I'm going to die," he wept.

"But why should you think such a thing? You have only a tummy bug, and the doctor will be here soon."

He shook his head, weeping into my bosom. "They made me . . . eat flowers," he said. "Poisonous flowers. They said I would die."

"What flowers?" I asked. "Who made you do this?"

"Yellow ones, the ones that grow near the chapel. They called me Daffy, and stood me on a table, and made me eat the flowers."

"Why?" I asked, alarmed at such a thing.

"Because I'm new, because . . . of my name. I don't know why, they hate me . . ."

"Who?" I asked. "Who did this horrible thing?"

He shook his head. "They made me swear not to tell . . . Please, please don't tell."

Doctor Cudgel arrived with his black bag, accompanied by Mr Talbot. He examined Adrian, taking a short history from him, wherein the child mentioned nothing about the forced ingestion of flowers. I hovered, knowing that I could not keep silent, yet unable to open my mouth if not addressed, and at the same time reluctant to betray the boy's confidence. The doctor gave the boy two injections, told me to increase his fluid intake, and to put a little salt and sugar in his water jug. Then he tousled the boy's head and told him not to worry, he would be back on the rugby field in no time. Torn, disturbed, I followed Mr Talbot and the doctor downstairs to the entrance hall. There I finally summoned the courage to tell them that Adrian – Flower, I corrected myself as Mr Talbot opened his mouth to admonish me again – had been forced to eat flowers, which might well have caused symptoms of poisoning and which could possibly herald worse consequences.

The two men stared at me.

"Impossible," declared Mr Talbot. "No boy here would do such a thing."

The doctor chuckled. "And if they did, it would be in jest. There is no flower here that could cause such severe symptoms! Go to bed," he added. "It's late, and tomorrow is another day."

"But, Doctor . . . " I tried again.

"Thank you for your help, Matron," Mr Talbot reinforced. "The boy will be fine."

The men strode away into the night, conversing about Frank Connell's ankle, and whether it would be ready in time for Saturday's match.

But I cannot sleep. I cannot sleep for fear of that boy next door all on his own, who will soon be released from my care. I cannot sleep for fear of what else might happen to him. Perhaps I should approach Father Nichols for guidance.

Lord, outside it is dark, and the sky black with cloud; the mountain is invisible.

⌇

Father Nichols made himself available to me today. I went to the rectory, and his maid brought us tea in the parlour. She then turned her attention to dusting the display cabinet, and I had the impression that she had been instructed to remain present, there being no Mrs Nichols. Indeed, Father Nichols seemed somewhat anxious finding himself seated opposite a lady, which might explain his ministry in a boys' school.

I introduced myself, and let him know I had been a member of Father Evans's parish. I then suggested that, since I ministered to the boys' physical well-being, and he to their spiritual, we should perhaps meet to discuss any scholars who might be cause for concern.

He seemed taken aback by this, and I realised with some embarrassment that I had ventured beyond my station. It only occurred to me then that there must already be channels in place to address such matters. I promptly made things worse by hurriedly bringing up the Flower affair as an example. Father Nichols trumpeted relief at this story, assuring me that, as I had had no children myself, let alone boy children, I would be unlikely to understand the nature of the pranks they get up to. He said he knew Flower, an overprotected boy, who could do with some toughening up. And what if there were to be another war? A man cannot allow minor irritants or emotional disturbances to sway him from the task at hand.

Can it be that I have overreacted? It is true that the world is a difficult place, and that too much emotion can interfere with the practicalities of life.

Yet I feel.

I don't know what I feel.

Unhappy.

Yet the good Lord has given me much, and these young men are privileged to be attending one of the best schools in the Union.

I will put my feelings aside. They have caused me grief in the past, and I will not allow them to undermine my new position.

⤚

Grace did not come to work today. Mrs Williams sent another girl, an African by the name of Elizabeth, to clean the sick bay and strip the beds. She kept shaking her head and clucking and sighing as she washed the windows, until I asked her what was wrong. She said that Grace's two-year-old son had died after a long illness.

Dear God. I am ashamed to say that in my shock, my first thoughts fell upon my own child. It has never before occurred to me that she may have died. Children are not supposed to die before their parents.

Why didn't Grace tell me? I think back on her flood of tears on knocking over the vase, and the missing medication, and I am horrified to think of this other matter that must surely have preoccupied her at the time.

I am in a torment again, despite the clear knowledge that You both give and take in Your own good time, and according to Your design.

I will give Grace a Bible if she does not already own one. I will remind her that her son is by Your side.

The night is long and cold and lonely. The weather squalls and rails like a giant child in a tantrum, wrenching the tall pines and hurling pails of rain against the window with the sound of thrown gravel. My chest is always at its worst when weather change is accompanied by anxiety. I am exhausted from lack of sleep and the effort of pulling air into and then pushing it out of my chest. I have used my pump so frequently that my hands shake, and my heart gallops in my ear.

Dear God, do not take me tonight. I am not so old, and my life feels unfinished. Wasted, actually. That poor two-year-old had no opportunity to develop his talents, and to serve You. His little body lies alone in the wet earth tonight and his mother's arms are empty.

What is it You want of me? This punishment of ill health is my due, I suppose, for wasting Your precious gift of life, for squandering it daily with sinful attitudes. Life-giving air is all around me, yet I cannot have it; my wilful body struggles against Your design.

It is pointless weeping. This is my fate, to be human and imperfect, and close to death. I do not wish to leave this room. I will return to bed and stay there until the end, until You come for me.

I wonder how my lion fares in this awful storm, whether he has adequate warmth and shelter, whether the air is kind to him. He has not lungs enough to roar against this mayhem.

Every breath, every sentence demands all I have.

If I died tonight they would find this journal. I must not die, please, God. Give me life, that I might live!

I must pull myself together, and try again tomorrow.

I have a plan in the event of my losing my job. I will approach my old employer, dear Mr Lawson; perhaps the situation at the pharmacy has changed and he could find a way to have me back in a full-time position, at a salary that could support me in some sort of boarding house.

Last night, as I feared would eventually happen, Mr Talbot entered the prep room to investigate the noise; he found me presiding over chaos. Harry Slater was amusing the others with wind noises he makes by cupping his palm beneath his armpit, and Simon Patterson had brought his pet mouse to prep and let it loose. I had for some time tried to persuade the boys to quieten down, and had failed. Now my employer stood at the door, and with one crack of the whip of his voice he had them all back at their desks, sitting still and straight. He glared at me, and told me, his voice booming in the hush, that he wanted to see me in his office tomorrow at three o'clock. Then he told the boys that if there was one more sound out of them, no one would be going home for the half-term break.

It is all very well for him – I do not have the authority to threaten them with this terrible penalty. Not going home.

The light recedes earlier each evening; Devil's Peak is silhouetted against a cold yet incandescent sky. A bold cerise is what is required, but the watercolours I can afford will not allow me to capture this. Yet these natural works of art are not meant to be captured; as I watch, the glow fades and is gone. Beauty cannot be held down.

I have tried to make this room my home. My parents gaze at me from the bedside table, as do You from the wall, Your kind face full of acceptance, despite all that befell You. I have brought some treasured things with me – Mummy's footstool, this fine tablecloth embroidered by my grandmother, my books. I was not permitted to bring Blackie. Phoebe managed to remove the Thomas Baines watercolour before the creditors moved in to Mummy's house, and now it apparently hangs in her hallway. We both loved it – the only thing of any real value.

At three o'clock tomorrow, all my faults will be examined. If I am found inadequate to this task, which at heart I know I am, I will lose even this.

I am not allowed to go home, to the house I lived in for fifty-four years, no matter how good my conduct, no matter how badly I fail at this job. I cannot even bear to take the train back to our old suburb, and to wander up the road to take a look, and to greet my beloved cat.

What if the new owners have altered the house? Besides, I am no longer welcome there, and it would break both my heart and Blackie's all over again. I must remain in this establishment for the December vacation, and make the best of it.

Yet You have told us that the only real home we have is at Your side in heaven. This is my comfort; this knowledge helps me to endure the unendurable.

⟜

To my surprise, Mr Talbot appeared courteous and almost friendly at our meeting. He even had the kitchen staff bring us some tea. I, however, was shaking like a schoolgirl called to the headmaster's office. I am embarrassed to say that I even managed to spill my tea, though fortunately only into my saucer. Now that I have recovered from my fright I realise how dreadful his recommendations are.

Mr Talbot says I am to send boys that misbehave in prep to the prefects' study for corporal punishment. I know the dictum – spare the rod and spoil the child – but I fear that Mr Talbot is doing this to teach me a lesson.

Last week I reported the incident concerning Derek Cameron to him. He is a boy who hails from Northern Rhodesia, unfortunate in that he must weigh nearly two hundred pounds and has a pink complexion. He was sent to the sick bay because the red stripes sliced across his behind prevented him from being able to sit at his desk. This was the work of one of the prefects, all of whom have the authority to punish new boys for misdemeanours. There are many rules a new boy must learn and obey, and, as a consequence, there are many transgressions.

I was shocked to see what had been done to Derek, and brought it to Mr Talbot's attention. He said he would look into it, and returned a while later to explain that the boy had been disobedient and cheeky, and needed to be put in his place. He said that in a school such as this, boys were sometimes pampered by indulgent, misguided mothers. Perhaps a little undue force had been used, but the boy had learnt a lesson, one that he would take seriously.

I am caught. I suspect it gives Mr Talbot some pleasure to see me struggle in his web.

It seems I must choose between losing this job and sending the boys for a beating.

Grace is back at work, and I do not know what to say to her. I decided not to cause her more upset by asking Mrs Williams to place her elsewhere in the boarding house. She goes about her duties quietly, and seems afraid of me, which, I must admit, suits me. We all have our troubles, and need not get involved in those of others. Elizabeth told me that Grace attends church, so she must have access to a Bible of sorts.

She is still young. Please, God, in Your good time, grant her and her husband another child.

I sent Harry Slater to the prefects yesterday during prep. He came back with such hatred on his face that I am afraid. But he has stopped making those noises. Young men must learn manners, I have decided. Especially in front of a lady.

I have not been able to put pen to paper for weeks.

The sick bay is full of snivelling and coughing boys. It is a wonder I have not succumbed. While I do feel ill, it is an emotional malaise.

I go about my day as usual, aware of a vague distress that I can't escape. It feels like a spiritual toothache, not confined to the mouth. I want to weep for the world, for these poor young creatures who do not have an inkling as to what has been sacrificed for them, and what is therefore required of them. They think that life can be cured with an aspirin, or that if one doesn't want to go to class, one can feign bellyache, or even a fever by dipping the thermometer into a cup of tea. They think that's all there is to it.

It was her birthday two weeks ago. I lit one candle for her, although there should have been thirty-eight. I have felt it in my body this time of the year, always, as though it were sewn in, a physical reminder. Every year I have carried it alone and silent – this grief. There has never been anyone to tell. Certainly not my parents, nor Phoebe, the only ones who knew what really happened. Other than Alan and his parents, possibly. On occasion I have considered unburdening myself to Ursula, but she sees me as a good person. I don't know how I could look her in the eye again if she knew.

At the time, everyone else was told, on the doctor's instructions, that I had been sent to Uncle Henry's farm on the northern border to overcome a touch of tuberculosis.

For four months I lived amongst thorn trees and dung beetles, next to a river alive with crocodiles. For four months, under Aunt Geraldine's eye, I waited, restless with the growing bulk and discomfort of life trapped inside me. Four months of waiting.

Animals would arrive to relieve the tedium: a warthog came to feed from the dog's bowl outside the kitchen door; a bird of paradise flitted erratically through the trees, collecting spider webs to bind its nest. The white splotches at the base of a tree revealed the perching place of the camouflaged pearlback owl above. Ouma, the kitchen girl who worked for Aunt Geraldine, showed me leopard spoor at the stream, and the consternation of a squirrel announced a python winding along a branch.

Afterwards, I was not allowed to see her. Our bodies wrenched and struggled for eighteen hours, trying to part. I have never felt such pain, nor do I ever wish to again. She did not want to be born; my body held her back. It was a torment, and I did not know how to end it. When she finally arrived, a nun put her calloused hand on my cheek and held my face to the wall as they bundled her up and took her away. But I heard her. I heard her cry out for me, and I felt my breasts respond. For days afterwards, my breasts hardened and wept a colourless fluid. For hours afterwards, I bled from between my shaking legs. I was terribly afraid. My body had been rent open, and I was certain I would die without her. Then they put me to sleep and sewed the tear closed. I came round, retching – but not even vomit would come out. I was closed, closed, shut to the world.

"Is she damaged?" I asked the nun who gave me tablets to ease the pain. Mummy had told me that my sin was twofold. As Alan was my cousin God would punish me with a malformed and retarded baby.

The nun was Irish, with a plain, scrubbed face. She hesitated, as though debating what to tell me. "She's lovely," she offered, confirming that she was a girl. "Don't you worry about her. She will make some childless couple very happy."

Yet I know that sometimes damage is all on the inside. I know that sometimes it isn't visible.

Aunt Geraldine put me on a train to Cape Town, back to my parents, back to my life.

As she stood outside my carriage window at the station, she patted my hand and told me I was a lucky girl. She said I could put this thing behind me now and start over again – that my life would not be destroyed.

I was sewn closed, so I wasn't able to tell her she was wrong. As the train puffed and jerked its way out of the station, impatient for Cape Town, I felt the tearing again. Later, it came to me: I'd left myself behind.

I didn't see Alan again. Everyone pretended nothing had happened. I went back to school to do the year over, and smiled and said I was better, thank you. My old friends had regrouped themselves, and my new classmates avoided me. They'd all heard about the TB. TB was what blacks got. TB was like leprosy. Peggy Saunders and her friends called me "wild stinking kaffir" for some time after that. I smiled and smiled and died. It didn't really matter, TB or pregnancy. This is what happens when you are rotten.

Soon after I'd returned home, the war ended. I was pleased for the world, but especially, I was glad for Alan, that he would not have to serve. I thought of phoning him, even though my parents had forbidden me to have any contact with him. Then one day I overheard my father as I laid the table for dinner. He was in the lounge having a drink with a friend, and I heard him announce proudly, as though speaking of the son he had never had, that Alan had won a scholarship to study at Oxford. He was to sail to England via the Suez Canal the following month.

The scattering, was the way I thought of it then. The pieces of me shattered, scattered across the earth.

⁓

Judy van Breda gave me a lift to the main road in her little Morris Minor today. Her parents must be moneyed for her to afford a car on a part-time librarian's salary. She has told me they live in a large house in Muizenberg, against the mountain.

I'd been on my way to the art-and-handcraft shop. When she found out about this, Judy was very enthusiastic and kindly invited me to her flat for a cup of tea and to show me her work. She has recently completed two large and impressive cross-stitch designs, one of the ruins of an English castle surrounded by spring flowers, and another of St George taking on a fiery dragon.

She is such a lovely young woman, in her late twenties, with a trim little figure. It makes me wonder that she hasn't found a nice young man to settle down with. The war took many of our best, and now women like her must struggle on without a husband. I must say, she does so cheerfully.

Later, as she drove me back to school, we passed the Prime Minister's residence. Four women dressed in black were standing outside with black sashes tied over one shoulder, their hands behind their backs, eyes cast down to the pavement in front of them. Judy pointed them out excitedly. They are apparently protesting against the proposed change to the constitution – a kind of vigil, or mourning, intended to embarrass the Nationalist government. I was astonished to see them, all respectable middle-aged women, standing in high heels in the heat.

One must strongly believe in something to do that, to put oneself on show in that way.

Of course, there are also those who like to be on show, and who would participate in these antics merely for effect. Phoebe is such a person. I can just see her, in a little black dress from Stuttafords, looking down at her Italian leather shoes outside Parliament.

No one would ever catch *me* making such a spectacle of myself!

～

Lord, please help me, guide me as to what to do. This afternoon I had a distinct impression that I was not the only person in the laundry room. It is an old section of the building, situated near the fire escape, and there are several nooks and crannies, as well as some large cupboards that extend to the ceiling. I had just stepped inside to fetch clean towels for the sick bay bathroom. As I took two towels from the pile, I heard a muffled sound. I decided not to investigate, as I have not yet managed to expurgate from my memory my indelicate encounter with those grappling boys.

On the other hand, I did not want to ignore the situation. Whoever it was, they were not supposed to be there. I called out: Who's there? which sounded ridiculous. So I retreated from the laundry room and took up a position at the elevated point where the stairs take a turn at the landing, out of sight of the laundry room door. And then I waited. Nothing happened for such a long time that I scolded myself for imagining things. Then the door opened tentatively, and Richard Jennings, a matric boy, emerged, glancing around. I was about to reveal myself in order to reprimand him for being out of bounds, when Grace followed. She looked as though she had been crying.

Rooted, I stood and watched as Richard turned to her and placed an open hand on her temple, and wiped away a tear beneath her eye with his thumb. The little coloured girl looked up into his eyes with an expression I have never seen on her face before; in fact, I realised then that she had never before looked directly at me. Yet here she was, staring with her brown eyes into Richard's face with such a look of hope and fear that I felt shocked. Then he brushed his lips against hers and strode away towards the common room. Grace, blowing her nose on a hanky, turned and went through the side door towards the scullery.

I am completely shaken. Stupid, stupid children! Though Grace is probably in her twenties, at least, and married at that, yet one never knows with these people.

Doesn't Richard realise what danger he puts himself in? Do the rich think they can get away with anything? There is the law that, rightly or wrongly, forbids even the act I witnessed. And should it get out of hand – if it hasn't already – it could ruin his life. Dear God, why do You insist on showing me things that are most inappropriate? Now that I have seen, I know – know what, exactly? Again I jump to conclusions . . . Still, I feel somehow implicated, responsible.

This has nothing to do with me!

I cannot rid my mind of the sight of the boy's white hand resting tenderly on that brown-skinned face.

It is ridiculous. I am the adult here, yet I cannot bring myself to talk to Grace. I am afraid I might make a fool of myself. Richard may simply have been taking something out of her eye. Perhaps it was co-incidence, their being in the laundry together, and they were hiding from me . . . there must be a hundred perfectly innocent explanations.

Yet I am very afraid that she has seduced him, looking for comfort, after her child's death. She doesn't care that she will ruin his life, and he is too stupid or rebellious to see what it is she does.

Unbeknown to her, I watched Grace making the beds today, and tried to imagine what Richard sees in her that he has even noticed her, let alone touched her. He can have anything he wants; the world is his. Whereas her world is as small as my thumbnail.

She has the high cheekbones and flattish eyes that one associates with the Hottentot – indeed, she would not look out of place in a loincloth, digging for roots. A hundred years ago, and that is where she would have been. Yet here she is in her blue maid's uniform mak-ing beds for rich young boys. She has been civilised to an extent, but what lies behind that guarded expression? What does Richard see? I cannot call her features beautiful, despite what one might, I suppose, describe as a sculpted face. As I looked, I noticed that she has a good figure. Nice straight teeth, too.

One forgets that these are young women, and should not really be employed in an establishment for young gentlemen. It is asking for trouble.

I am very upset and unsettled by all this. I will speak to Father Evans during the vacation. He will guide me. Father Nichols is closer at hand, but he looks at me with suspicion, as though I am Eve about to dangle an apple in front of him.

In the meanwhile, painting will help me. Painting, and a visit to the garden, where the daisies are in such abundance that they make me want to laugh out loud.

What fun I had today! After breakfast I was released, it being a Saturday, with no boys in the sick bay. Judy, bless her, invited me to a Gilbert and Sullivan at the Labia Theatre; she had complimentary tickets as her brother is in it. She suggested that we go into town in the afternoon for a bit of window-shopping and tea before the matinée. I agreed, not wishing to appear niggardly, even though I was worried about the extra costs of such an outing.

It is years since I have been in the centre of town, and I was enthralled by the bustle. We parked on the Parade, and first we wandered around the market, its tables arrayed with fruit and fabric and bric-a-brac. Judy warned me to hold onto my bag tightly, which I did among all those purse snatchers. We were regaled by a lay preacher turned madman – or the other way round – standing on his box and prophesying the end of the world. He was unkempt, yet had an extraordinary face – like that, I imagined, of an Old Testament prophet, with long hair and a beard, and staring eyes that appeared to see the Apocalypse. I would have loved to paint him. Mad as he was, he had some pertinent things to say about our sinful and wayward natures. He looked as if he were homeless, and I wondered about his family. Nobody except me appeared to be listening to him.

A young coloured girl of about ten then caught my eye. She was peeling the crusts off her sandwich and feeding them to the pigeons that rose and fell around us with an agitation of wings, competing for the spoils. She had a face so pure it was almost featureless, with plaits on either side of it. Her mother called, and she ran off to help her carry parcels. Please, God, I prayed as she glanced up into her mother's face, please spare her.

A woman a little older than me was rooting around on a table strewn with second-hand bric-a-brac. She was down at heel, her face worn with worry. She asked the price of a brass doorknob, then replaced it, shaking her head. It was not costly, but she could clearly not afford it.

Judy was bargaining with a coloured woman who was selling gorgeous fabrics. She had an open face; a young child in a threadbare shirt hung onto her skirts, and stared up at me with a face smeared with the remains of a cold. I wished that Judy would not haggle so, and was relieved when she stopped and walked on without the material. On glancing over my shoulder, I saw the young child, of indeterminate sex, still staring agape after me.

We then went to have tea upstairs at Stuttafords, which I had visited only once before, with Ursula; I feel out of place amongst such finery. Mummy scorned the rich. She asked why we should fraternise with them here on earth, when Jesus told us they would not enter heaven; so fat and acquisitive, the rich were far less likely than camels to fit through the eye of heaven's needle. Yet the immaculately dressed woman who sat at the next table was nice enough to her little boy who was enjoying a cream soda, and I saw her leave the waitress a large tip.

Judy must surely be moneyed, despite her job – which she clearly does simply because she loves it. Without a second thought, she bought herself an exquisite dress that she spotted on the way out of Stuttafords. I had to struggle with and overcome the sin of envy, and I complimented her on her purchase.

The opera was a treat, yet I was distracted by thoughts of all the lives I had brushed against that afternoon, all the varied lives I might have been destined to lead, in different circumstances. Yet You, in Your infinite wisdom, have given me this life, Lord. What shall I make of it? Is it too late?

Even as I watched the singers on stage, and laughed at their antics, I could feel the corners of my tacked-down life starting to come away. I shy away from what lies below. There is a terrible darkness in me. Please, God, shine Your light into every living crevice, so that I will be fit to do Your duty. Help me be Your immaculate servant, perfect in Your sight.

The sick bay is full of boys with sore stomachs and migraine. Mrs Calitz tells me this is typical of the time of the year as exam tension builds. She says I should turf them all out, and stop pandering to them. But I look at their pale, strained faces, and my heart goes out to them. The world is such a demanding place. I will leave it to Doctor Cudgel's decision – who is to go back to class and who will stay in bed.

Last week the doctor referred to the state of my chest, which has in fact been much better recently – not that he would know, for it is in the early hours of the morning that I am really troubled. I quickly reassured him that I was on medication, and that all was well. He suggested a chest X-ray. I know what he refers to. The scourge of TB, so common amongst the poor. Through his eyes I am, despite my whiteness, poor; a woman of any means whatever would not be in my position. So I have agreed to go up to Groote Schuur Hospital next week.

Ironically, the doctor's concern has aggravated my condition. Anxiety goes straight to my airways, clamping them, since once, long ago, I was regarded as an unclean TB sufferer. Life appears to be constructed in a series of loops – one returns repeatedly to certain disagreeable themes.

Perhaps this time I will indeed be shown to have that dreadful disease. It was a killer in the time of the great poets, but in this modern era of antibiotics, the worst that could happen is that I lose my employment.

I don't want to go and I don't want to stay. Such contrariness belongs to a child. What will become of me? Ursula has offered me accommodation for the summer holidays, but then I will have to put up with her wretched dogs and her recurrent complaints about George. Of course, I could stay in the boarding house after the boys have gone. Six weeks! I have never spent so much time on my own, but it should be better in the summer. There are masters who live on the grounds, so I would not be entirely alone.

Then Judy van Breda said she was going to stay with her parents in Muizenberg, and would I come and visit. I said I would, not wanting to offend, but as usual I have made the offence worse, for I cannot go. I must find some suitable excuse, for I cannot confess that the ghosts of my childhood inhabit that very stretch of coastline. I have not returned there for forty years. Forty years is half a lifetime.

I wonder when I will die.

The X-ray was clear, so it shouldn't be of TB.

Rory is a shocking man. I ought to have nothing to do with him. He asked me whether I had ever walked up Devil's Peak. Well, of course not, but he implied that it would be an interesting thing for me to do, seeing that the mountain is my model, or subject matter. When I expressed reservations, for it is a very high mountain and I am more accustomed to walking along flat areas, he went on to say that the old masters knew their subjects very well. He was implying that they all had intimate relations with their models.

Why does he provoke me so? It is a terrible and untrue analogy on several counts. He is obsessed with sex, and I will avoid him from now on.

Besides, I have learnt that there is no Mrs McCullough.

⌒

It is very quiet. All was in a tumult yesterday as the boys prepared to leave. I looked at their ebullient faces and understood: they were returning to their real lives. The labelled suitcases lined up in the hall were destined for their real homes, where their real mothers would welcome them, and unpack and wash their clothes, and bring them hot cocoa in bed in the mornings.

I have done my best, but they are leaving me. Only one boy, only one, pressed a card into my hand, and hugged me goodbye when no one else was looking. Adrian Flower, who wrote in a crushed and awkward script: "Thanks, Matron! Ta ta till next year!" Even as he handed it to me, I saw that he had already turned away, dreaming of another place I have no knowledge of.

Another shock. The Talbots are going to America. Mrs Talbot, at high table the other evening, exclaimed at my decision to stay on at the school over the break. "You have no family?" she demanded. Well, yes, I do, but there has been no word from Phoebe since I ignored her petition. And my elderly aunt in Rustenburg is not someone I would want to visit, even if I could afford it. Aunt Geraldine went back to England after Uncle Henry passed away. And Alan's family has not spoken to me since I was sixteen.

Not that I admitted any of this to Mrs Talbot, about to flounce off across the world on her high heels. Perhaps she will fall off one of them and break an ankle, and ruin her whole trip. What I did say to her, with a subtle air of mystery, is that I am busy on certain projects – and then I refused to elaborate. That will give her something to think about. That might shut her up.

Last night I had to fight nightmares to do with carnivorous fish and a slave whose wrists were pegged high onto an old stone wall. I even kept the light on, though it did occur to me that any malevolent person could then identify exactly which part of the building is still occupied.

This is the problem of having a wild imagination, which is the consequence of never really having grown up. Children are afraid of the night and monsters under the bed and suchlike, and I must repeatedly remind myself that I am an adult; also that there is no real danger. Mrs Williams is still about in her room at the other end of the house, and Mr Leighton skulks around somewhere. Father Nichols and his housekeeper are also still resident on the grounds. None of them provide company, but at least I am not alone. If I were to attract any trouble, I am certain they would help me.

⌐⌐

It's a girl, poor thing. The baby bears no resemblance to either parent, in my view. But then newborn babies hardly look human, all emaciated and hirsute, with their twiggy little fingers. Phoebe is all a-gush in the letter that accompanies the photograph, going on and on about how long and difficult the labour was. Well, what does she expect? Labour is not called that for nothing! She has always talked about her experiences of pregnancy and childbirth as if I know absolutely nothing about the subject. And now, with this grandchild, there will be much gloating and carrying on.

I suppose I will have to send a present to little Sheila, which is what the parents have called her. In that household, she will already have been given everything one could think of, and I am expected to spend my hard-earned money on something that will not be appreciated; all for the child of a nephew I have never had the proper opportunity of getting to know.

To think, Phoebe is now a grandmother. Granny Phoebe.

It sounds ridiculous.

⌐⌐

It is my own fault. I could be elsewhere, but I chose to stay here, thinking I would paint and garden and read.

Instead I potter, pretending to be busy, but all I achieve by the end of the day is the putting down of a hem and washing the curtains which do not, in all honesty, need washing again so soon. I cannot be idle, for I feel Satan's breath on my shoulder. I have even scrubbed the sick bay floor so as to eliminate the accretion of germs that have most certainly survived Grace's rudimentary efforts. I have tried to impress on her the importance of cleanliness, particularly in a place where the sick are cared for, but she merely averts her eyes, and nods, and goes about her work in exactly the same manner she has always done.

Perhaps the problem is one of language, for my Afrikaans is not very good. Of course, she could be stupid, though I have on occasion seen her reading the newspaper in the common room. Last week, when I came upon her leaning over the paper on the table instead of doing her work, she did have the decency to look guilty, and returned immediately to her sweeping. I went straight to the page she had open, and saw an article about the Black Sash – as the women Phoebe has joined call themselves. Adjacent to the article was a photograph of two rows of women dressed in black and facing each other on either side of the DF Malan airport doors, forming a short corridor. They are wearing their sashes, and are standing in their usual pose, staring down at the ground in front of them, while a bemused Minister Schoeman walks between them.

I'd glanced at Grace, busy banging around with the broom – why is it that she must make so much noise? – and wanted to ask her what she understood of all this, and whether it affected her. Coloured women do not have the vote; it is only coloured men whose right to vote will be rescinded, should the Act be passed. But if I'd begun that conversation with her, where would it have led? If you put certain thoughts into people's heads, it is bound to make them unhappy.

I have not managed to say anything to her about her son, either, and I cannot think why. There is a thickness in the air between us that is impenetrable, so we largely ignore each other. It might be better that way.

Then there is that other matter. Richard has fortunately matriculated, and gone home to the Transvaal, out of harm's way. What Grace feels about this is not apparent. Since that episode in the laundry room, I find I cannot stop looking at her.

Anyway, Grace is going on leave tomorrow, thankfully, so for a while I will not have to respond to her or to anyone else's presence.

⟅⟆

The chapel is a consolation to me at times like these. It is a place I can go to when there is no other. Not even Father Nichols is around, now that it is vacation time, though he does live on the premises. One would think that he would on occasion visit Your house for prayer.

I know, Lord, that I am unworthy. I am like a germ in the healing hospital of Your great love. I am dirt before the sanctity of Your house of worship. Please, God, forgive me, cleanse me of all evil thoughts and deeds.

I do not want to make excuses, but the irony is that my latest sin arose from a good intention. There are some pot plants in the standard seven dormitory that belong to an unpopular boy, Stephen Parsons, who is nicknamed Parsley, and whose only apparent crime is that he wears spectacles and loves plants, and who, I am certain, is destined to become a great botanist. He asked me to tend the plants while he was in Southern Rhodesia, and I willingly agreed. There is nothing that upsets me more than the thought of something trapped – like an animal in a cage or a plant in a pot – and withering away because of human neglect. So I was in the dormitory last week watering the fuchsia and the impatiens he has successfully grown from slips, which have transformed his corner of the room, but about which he is mercilessly teased.

It was a lovely day, slightly too hot for my liking, but a welcome relief from the grey, chest-clutching cold of the Cape winters. Standing at the window as I was, I naturally looked outside. The standard seven dormitory is on the first floor facing south, and the view looks over a wall, onto the swimming pool. I was not expecting to see anyone there, other than Mr Jansen or Samuel, possibly, who look after the grounds. But sitting on the edge of the pool, deep in conversation, were two naked boys. In my shocked state, I must confess I did not immediately turn away as I should have. My eyes are not as good as they were, so I did not recognise the boys' faces at that distance. I assumed they must be day scholars who had illegally ventured onto school property during vacation time to alleviate the heat.

Please, God, forgive me, but I could not stop watching them as they sunned and swam, unashamed, unself-conscious. Their bodies, You see, I found very beautiful. Is that wrong? You have created our bodies, just as You have created delicate, long-stemmed flowers and the sombre mountain with its deep folds, and I stood a long while that afternoon appreciating the miracle of Your creation. I also wept, as I stood there. I loved Alan, even though I know it was wrong. I loved to watch his graceful, supple body under the full embrace of the sun at a time when I thought that anything was possible, and that love would find a way past any difficulty. I sinned again and again, taking beauty for myself, feeling that I was making a miracle out of my dour life. It felt like a blessing. I was wrong, wrong, and yet I must confess to feeling still that it was the best time of my life.

Even after all that transpired, I am ashamed to admit that I still would not refuse him.

The truth is, I am still sixteen years old. I have not grown up. I still want the same things a wayward young girl would want, I am still a stupid girl resident in an ageing woman's body.

I realised later that if someone had come along and found me at the window occupied in such a manner, they would have used a certain term to describe me, a terrible word that I cannot accept. Life is confusing, Lord, and I am in constant need of Your forgiveness.

The floor of the chapel is very hard on my knees, but I have decided I will not use the cushions provided to relieve my suffering. I will not forget: for a short indulgence in pleasure, one must endure a lifetime of pain.

⤸

Lord, I had to get out. I only pray I have not leapt from the frying pan into the fire.

Rory has been working in the art room on paintings for an exhibition, taking the opportunity of the vacation for some concentrated work. I have been bringing him coffee and scones I baked myself in the school kitchens, for although he can be outrageous, even offensive, there is something about his boyish manner that I find endearing. I think he likes to shock me because he wants to find out exactly how prudish I am, and I refuse to play the part.

I am also grateful that he has taken the time to offer me this strange friendship. I cannot entirely shake off the suspicion that he does so for some dark motive, for why else would any male befriend the likes of me?

Besides, I am lonely, if truth be told. I don't even know where I am going to be for Christmas. It is the celebration of Your birth, Lord, but for me it is also that most difficult of times.

I like to watch Rory work. He is most unorthodox, and will often use unusual objects to paint with – his knuckles, a stick, a piece of crumpled newspaper, or an old rag. He will apply paint to the canvas, and then, from across the room, sit back, chain-smoking, and stare at the painting like an interrogator patiently waiting to extract the truth from an unwilling subject. At times like these he forgets that I am in the room. It is truly astonishing that he allows me to watch. I would get stage fright and be unable to continue.

Though at times becoming bored with waiting for his next move, I remain still so as not to interrupt his concentration. Sometimes I am so reluctant to change position that I find my leg has gone numb. I have noticed, though, that when Rory finally stands up and approaches the canvas, the mark he makes never fails to astonish me. It is never what I expect. At times his marks are lyrical, but at others

I want to cry out to prevent him from interfering further with a certain perfect part of the canvas. My judgment is clearly out of kilter, facile and ill-educated. He inhabits a world so different from mine it is a miracle we can even converse.

Today he came to an abrupt halt in the midst of reworking a surface, threw his brush into a jar of turpentine and wiped his paint-stained hands on his trousers. He took a last look at his painting, then swung round to me and pinned me with his shocking blue eyes.

"Come," he commanded, "I've had enough. We are going up the mountain." I objected, clutched with worry. My walking shoes were not designed to deal with rough or steep terrain, but he reassured me that the knee he'd damaged in the war was bothering him, so we would not be planting flags on the summit today.

There is that other worry of being alone with a male person. But I know I am being silly. Rory could not possibly have designs on a frumpish spinster at least ten years older than he. So I packed a tea and we set off to Rhodes Memorial in his Austin. As we drove through the gate near the university, I was aware of passing close by Alan, and also of the proximity of my lion in the zoological gardens. I have never visited either place. Tears of self-pity pricked and threatened, though I fortunately managed to contain them.

Today is Saturday, so Rhodes Memorial was full of picnickers and holidaymakers admiring not only the view across the peninsula to the Hottentots Holland mountains, but also the impressive architecture of the Memorial building. It was good to be out and to feel part of the goings-on of the world, so I was grateful to Rory for this expedition, and put my melancholia behind me.

I remember, as a child, visiting the Memorial with Father soon after it was opened in 1912. It was one of his favourite places to have a picnic tea, especially when entertaining business visitors from countries up north. The statues of the lions and the horse rider and the bust of Cecil John Rhodes himself are inspiring. So, too, is the inscription below the bronze head – an extract from a poem by Rhodes's friend, Rudyard Kipling, written specially for the great man:

> The immense and brooding spirit still
> Shall quicken and control.
> Living he was the land, and dead,
> His soul shall be her soul.

Some of us are born for great things, Lord. That must surely be an easier life – to know what you are born for, to have great visions and plans. Rory snorted when I voiced this. He said Rhodes was a crook who deceived not only farmers around Kimberley to profit from diamonds, but also Lobengula to gain control of Southern Rhodesia for the British Empire.

Well, I couldn't argue with him, being unschooled in history, but I do have Father's word for it that Rhodes was an honourable man. I felt quite upset by Rory's declaration, and if I could have abandoned the walk and retired to my room, I would have done so. But there we were, against my better judgment, and I was forced to pretend that all was well, and that I was enjoying the afternoon.

I suspect some people enjoy destroying the reputations of others. Rory will never be a Cecil John Rhodes, not even in the field of art, so I imagine his slight is fuelled by his own insecurities and failures.

Talking thus to myself, I managed to regain some of my earlier good humour.

Despite his damaged leg, Rory set off up the path at quite a pace, and at one point I had to ask him to slow down. On reaching the track that runs along a contour of the mountain, we walked for a while side by side. The vegetation was looking particularly pretty, with ericas in bloom, and there was a haze over Table Bay that made it look like a painting by Turner, which I commented on, but received no response. Rory appeared preoccupied, and I worried for a while that I had offended him. After some time, though, he said he was still mulling over the painting he had abandoned – he'd not been able to put it out of his mind. Then, with what seemed a great effort of will, he asked me whether my subject was as interesting close up as from far. I had a suspicion he was teasing me, but had decided that he was not going to upset me on this splendid afternoon, with my chest open and clear as a flue. I replied that even good artists had only a partial view of the Creation, but that our escapade – the word slipped out, and I was immediately concerned that it did not convey my intended meaning – would no doubt allow me to take further mental notes.

He raised an eyebrow, and asked me, since he had gone to the trouble of bringing me up close to my subject for this view of it, whether I would bring him up close to my paintings?

Intending to entertain, I replied, "When pink elephants take to the sky," but he seemed to lose interest, and our walk ended quite abruptly and silently. I worried all the way home that I had bored him.

I was glad to be back safe in my little room, and discovered that I was longing to pick up my brushes, which I did, and ended up painting long after the light had disappeared, and with it, my subject. I painted from memory, and made up things I have never seen, and before long the peak had a strange tilt and glow to it, as though goblins resided below.

The painting is not realistic, and I would rather die than show it to anyone, but I must say I am very pleased with it.

⌒

I did not have the heart to make excuses in the face of Judy's insistence, and now I am duty-bound to spend Christmas with the Van Breda family. Lord, this is Your doing. What am I to understand by it?

It struck me yesterday that Alan may possibly be staying in his parents' holiday house in Muizenberg.

What is the use! Why do I torture myself with these stupid thoughts?

A wagtail has befriended me in the silence of the days. This could never have happened when Blackie was with me, as he was such an adept hunter. This wagtail is at my windowsill now, an amusing reminder of how the tail can wag the dog, his body bobbing, looking for the crumbs I put out daily, and for flies trapped behind the glass. He seems to have no fear; his confidence is a wonder. Have You sent him to me to teach me this?

I will approach Your birthday with the attitude of the wagtail, even though fear sits in my throat like vomit. I will go out and reclaim the world, even though I would rather hide in my bed and weep.

⌒

I was sitting at my table a little earlier today, pondering a few things. Why, for example, does Ursula – having invited me to stay – now tell me she is off with her dogs to Herold's Bay to stay with her friend Fran? I suspect she has done this on purpose to hurt me, for I let slip that Judy invited me for Christmas. Ursula cannot abide my having other friends. I don't know what to do about her; and this, after all I have been through with her. At least, though, she will be away from George for a while, and she'll have to complain into someone else's ear.

As I sat enveloped in these thoughts, I saw the strangest thing: a small pink elephant with floppy ears popped into view at the window! It was a cardboard cut-out, of course, held aloft by the dear art teacher on one of those long hooked poles meant for opening windows. I flung the sash open, and laughed down at him. Rory is such a delightful rogue!

"Come on!" he said. "You promised!"

I had him up for tea, but managed to withstand his pleas. Why would he want to look? It would only end in embarrassment for both of us.

He told me he would be visiting friends in the Karoo for Christmas. In this heat! I must confess, Lord, that I will miss him. Everyone is going away.

I have been wondering whether I should give Rory a gift for Christmas, but I am afraid he might misunderstand. Then, of course, what to give him? I had the mad idea to give him one of my watercolours, but that is unthinkable.

Mrs Williams is off to a niece in Wellington, and Father Nichols is going to Somerset West to preach in a parish there.

I cannot bear to stay here with only Mr Leighton around, and look forward to Tuesday when I will set off to catch the train.

Lord, please send me a sign. If it is Thy will, I am prepared to take my courage in hand. I will walk up the steps leading to Alan's front door, raise my knuckles, and knock.

How is it that the past takes certain places hostage? That smells and sounds and buildings so strongly attach themselves to past events and feelings, it is as though they are melded into one thing.

The last stretch of railway that runs past the vlei before the sea comes into view was an agony that summer. I longed to see him, but was worried he would not be at Muizenberg Station to meet me, having surely found something better to do than meet his little cousin. As though intending to prolong my fever, the train slowed down well before reaching the station. I could hardly remember what he looked like from the year before. As we approached the station, Phoebe already had her head sticking out of the window, taking up all the space, so I jostled in next to her, trying to establish my position as the older sister, craning my neck to see if he were there.

"For goodness' sake, sit down, Phyllis!" my mother commanded. "Stop making an exhibition of yourself! You'll soon cause an accident." So Phoebe was the first to see him and to wave a greeting.

He had suddenly become older, turned from a boy to a man in one year. I was struck dumb, and smiled foolishly, not knowing where or how to position my hands. He pecked my exclaiming mother on the cheek, nodded a shy greeting at us two girls, then took a suitcase in each hand and led us down the steps towards the promenade opposite his parents' holiday house. I can still see the back of his neck, the flange of muscle spreading down under his collar to his shoulders, tensed with the effort of our luggage. Phoebe skipped beside him, chattering about this and that. I sauntered along, hoping to provide a contrasting image of maturity and composure. He would tire of her soon, I felt sure.

Father was away in German South West Africa as part of the war effort, but he joined us a few days later, by which time Phoebe had come down with a fever and a sore throat and was not allowed outside, much to my satisfaction. Uncle Jack and Father spent the vacation fishing and listening to news of the war on the wireless, while Aunt Joan and Mummy cooked and swam and went for tea and played bridge at other people's houses. Often, in the evenings, the adults got dressed up and went off in Uncle Jack's Ford to the dance hall in Kalk Bay, where the officers from Simon's Town naval base also took time off to relax. So, we children were left pretty much to our own devices.

Phoebe turned out to have glandular fever, and had to rest as much as possible. Mummy tried to make me play nursemaid to her, but after getting her some books from the library, I went off with Alan. We swam and covered each other in sand and sculpted sandcastles, and after Christmas we carried his new canoe down to the mouth of the vlei and paddled upstream to where birds nested in the reeds, and watched flocks of flamingos come and go. We explored a small bushy island in the middle of the expanse of water, pretending we were castaways from the world who had escaped the hard reality of war. We sat eating sandwiches while the water slapped and rippled, and talked about the war, and whether Alan would have to sign up when he finished school the following year, or whether it would all be over by then.

For the first time in my life, my body felt like a shimmering garment, glazed and burnished by the sun, and also by Alan's warm gaze. I felt filled with life, and with desire for still more of it. For the first time ever I felt that I was wanted.

This morning, as the train passed the vlei, I felt the same shiver in my marrow as when I was fifteen, as though there was something, someone to anticipate – but this was followed by crushing grief. Judy met me at the station, and wanted to know what was wrong. I wish I could tell her. I wish I could explain this pain even to myself. It all happened so long ago, in another life.

Judy's parents' double storey is nearer to the mountain than the beach, so we did not pass close to Alan's house. Mr and Mrs van Breda have made me feel very welcome, and I have a lovely room upstairs under the eaves, with a window that looks out over False Bay, where the waves pleat themselves endlessly onto the shore.

After lunch, the two of us walked a little way up Muizenberg Peak, and had tea from a thermos flask, with some home-made chocolate biscuits. Fortunately, Judy was very talkative, telling me about the book she is reading – a Virginia Woolf she thinks I will enjoy. Then she proceeded to tell me about her childhood here, so I did not need to contribute much to the conversation.

To think, she'd not even been born that summer. This librarian is younger, even, than my daughter.

It is still there, and looks the same but for a couple of features. The balcony has been glassed in against the southeaster – a good idea, as the wind is unremitting at this time of the year. The palms Uncle Jack planted either side of the gate are now three times my height, and I was surprised to see that the grassy area in front of the house has been paved in.

We passed the house today on the way to the beach for a swim, and then again on the way back. There was no sign of life either inside the house or in the garden, other than a tabby cat that refused my entreaties. He is probably away for the holidays with his family. I imagine a bold but affectionate woman of good proportions who adores her three children, and who does not begin to suspect that they have a half-sister somewhere else. Alan would never have told her about me.

Tomorrow is my birthday. I have not mentioned this to anyone. Only Ursula might remember, and she has no way of contacting me. It was on a night like this that Alan first kissed me: happy birthday, and on the lips.

Tomorrow, when we go again to swim, what should I make of it if You should position Alan in his garden, or at the window, dear Lord? Am I to look the other way, or must I open his gate and go to greet him? What then of his unsuspecting wife?

Would there be anything left of the tenderness I felt in Alan's caress, or would he turn away from me, his eyes widening with horror?

I have been given a double bed here, and it is the first time I have slept in one, apart from those times with Mummy towards the end. I anticipated it being a luxury, a stretching out of one's body between sheets of real linen. But I have found it to be a heartache, and lonely, at that.

⟋

Judy is a kind and observant soul – she has noticed how the house captures my attention each time we pass. She probed gently, and I confessed that I knew the owners in my youth, and had wondered who lives there now. She did not know, but asked her mother, who is very sociable in the area. To my relief and sorrow, Mrs van Breda informed us that as far back as she can remember, there has only been a Mr Porter and his family living there.

Why did Uncle Jack sell? He and Aunt Joan loved it here – they'd in fact mentioned that they intended to retire to this very house. Perhaps this place was too hard for any of us to bear after my dreadful error.

Thank God I had the presence of mind to bring my journal with me, for I cannot sleep. Outside in the night, the ocean breathes its tides in and out under a sliver of moon; the sighs of the waves ride in over the windowsill.

I shouldn't have come here, it was against my better judgment, but now I will just have to make the best of it.

1956

It is the New Year, and heat lies like a thick woollen blanket on the land. The sallow grass crushes crisply beneath my tread, and the bushes wilt, despite Samuel's ministrations. Not a cloud in sight.

Rory has suggested another outing to the mountain, but I have declined in this heat. I would rather sit with my book and my journal during these last few days before the boarders return and the hubbub recommences. I have become quite fond of being quietly by myself during the daylight hours. It is during the nights that I would prefer company, even that of sick boys.

I sometimes have a strange calm in me, which I would retain and nurture, but before too long it gives way to the edges of anxiety, as though a storm is brewing just beyond the horizon. Of course, it might only be the thought of the return of the boys. But in this state my mind swivels between thoughts of Mummy and the terrible life she had, and thoughts of Alan and our daughter, both forever lost to me; and then darkness swills around my heels and all peace departs.

The novel in my lap offers a safe haven. Yet I know that it will come to an end and leave me facing myself. All books, including the Bible, provide a brief respite from myself. Like doors opening, books show me other places, other people, other lives. But books close again, and I am locked back into myself, the key thrown, gone.

Dear Lord, in Your wisdom, please grant me the peace of mind of knowing what has become of her. Please, Lord, let her life turn out differently to mine.

⌒

What an interesting evening! I feel like a young girl again!

When Rory invited me to his flat for dinner, I initially declined, giving my lack of transport as a reason. He brushed all objections aside, though, and came to fetch me this evening at six o'clock. I imagined, as I escaped with Rory in his Austin, that Mrs Williams, Father Nichol and Mrs Talbot were all peering out of their respective abodes at this scandal, and for one mad moment I wanted to shriek "Good riddance!" from the car window.

He lives in an old apartment block in Tamboerskloof, which he shares with an Afrikaans friend he'd once mentioned, Pierre van der Something, I cannot quite remember his surname. He is an older man of about my age, with a full head of white hair and spectacles that frame doe eyes. He gesticulates and laughs a lot, particularly at his own jokes, but perhaps that is all right as he can be very amusing.

Rory introduced me to Pierre in the most flattering terms, saying how kind I am. Pierre is flourishingly gallant, and took my hand and pressed his lips to it for a moment longer than is perhaps acceptable, leaving a damp patch on the back of it. He exclaimed that Rory had told him what a hard life I'd had; also, he remarked that I had obviously been beautiful in my youth, and that there is still much to be admired in the lines of my face! Later, after dinner, he insisted I make an appointment at his salon in Sea Point so that he can do my hair. He said he would show me how to style it. I dared not confess that I have only been into a hairdresser for the occasional trim since Mummy became too frail to cut my hair for me. In our family, hairdressers have always been regarded as an indulgent waste of money.

What to do? Pierre has offered me a perm, free of charge! I am so used to the practical way I manage my hair, clipped to one side, that the thought scares me. I might end up looking like Phoebe! And surely, to wear a perm, one needs fashionable clothes to complement it. Besides, I cannot possibly get all the way to Sea Point.

However, if Pierre is as good a hairdresser as he is a cook, I should not turn the offer down too quickly. He produced a delicious dish called "cockohva" – he said it was French – followed by a marvellous baked Alaska. I joked with him that he had taken me on a culinary tour of the world. Rory took this as a cue to bring out the port wine he says is from Portugal, and then he and Pierre treated themselves to Cuban cigars on the balcony, on account of my chest. It was lovely sitting out in the night air, overlooking the city and harbour strung with lights illuminating ships from all over the world. There was only one moment I worried that the evening might be spoilt. Rory spoke about a friend who had recently returned from America. She'd told him about a Negro woman in Alabama who had been arrested for refusing to give up her bus seat to a younger white man, and to sit in the back section reserved for Negroes. Her action had sparked a state-wide bus boycott.

Rory was furious that this news had not been printed in our papers, but Pierre rebuked him, asking whether he really wanted our country to go up in flames. Rory then went on in his usual fashion about how it was about time the Africans in the Union objected to discrimination – for hadn't there just been a world war about precisely that issue? Pierre said he had had enough of war, thank you very much.

I agree with Pierre – I find even arguments most disagreeable. I am pleased to say I saved the occasion by interjecting that the two of them sounded like an old married couple, which reduced them to tears of mirth. I don't know why they found this so funny, but it allowed me to change the subject. I could hear music playing in a downstairs flat – a Vera Lynn tune from the time of the Great War that my parents had loved very much. I told them that it released a mixture of happiness and sadness in me, stirring up all the sediment from that time.

At this, Rory shot up, exclaiming about a record his friend had brought from America as a gift. It was a new release by a man called Elvis Presley. Before I knew it, Rory had pushed back the chairs in the sitting room, rolled up the carpet and lowered the needle onto the record. As the music started, he pulled me into the middle of the room and began jigging and twisting about to a sound I had never before heard the likes of. Was this Negro music? I have heard the blues before, but this was not ordinary blues. It certainly had a good rhythm, so I bravely did my best, spurred on by the headiness of male company and over-indulgence – sherry followed by port makes one quite merry. Then Pierre joined us and I found myself, rather curiously, dancing with two men in a kind of triangle. I was aware that if a neighbour had looked in it would have been a strange sight. When a slow song came on, Pierre performed a little bow, inviting me to dance with him. As though on cue, Rory promptly retired to an armchair, pretending, I thought, to be worn out.

What was I to do? It has been such a long time since I've been close to any man. Pierre gripped me to himself, and I inhaled the strange and alarming smell of the male. As we moved to the rhythm of the music, over his shoulder I saw Rory watching us, his arms thrown back, with his hands clasped behind his neck. The expression on his face was so full of sad longing that I did not know what to think.

> Well, since my baby left me
> I've found a new place to dwell.
> It's down at the end of Lonely Street
> At Heartbreak Hotel.

Rory suggested I spend the night and that I could sleep in his bedroom. He said he didn't mind sharing with Pierre, and in the morning we could take a picnic breakfast to Bantry Bay. But I couldn't possibly have done that – what would the staff think if I spent the night out at a man's residence! I was embarrassed to ask Rory to take me all the way back to the school again – it was already after twelve.

I must say that I was a little afraid Rory might try to kiss me when he dropped me off at the school, so I leapt out of the car, gushing my thanks a little too enthusiastically. He nodded slightly, and smiled, his elbow resting on the frame of the open car window, and said he would see me on Monday. Again, he looked so sad, I was worried I had offended him.

It seems to me that we are all caught up in some private drama.

It is late. I have foolishly spent some time in front of the mirror, trying to find what it was that Pierre had seen in my face. I decided, eventually, that he was merely being kind to his friend's friend. That sort of kindness cannot be trusted.

～

The cold light of day brings one down with a bump. I am so unused to social discourse that I have difficulty most of the time understanding what is really going on. Was Rory matchmaking? Was he perhaps concerned about my intentions, and therefore trying to pass me on to Pierre?

How embarrassing.

Anyway, what is wrong with these two eligible bachelors, that they have not married in a time when there is a surfeit of women?

Pierre is a good all-rounder, and would be a welcome gift to most women, but he simply does not appeal to me. What is wrong with me, Lord? It appears that the imprint Alan left on my young soul has spoilt me for any other man. Even Hugo, poor Hugo! He was no real match for my one, true love. To be honest, it was not only because of Mummy that I turned Hugo away.

How to clarify matters with Rory? What lay in that sad look? My impulse is to comfort him, but then he might misinterpret even that.

Last night was the first time I have been held close since I was a girl. Hugo was not the type to embrace one, let alone dance. It is a miracle he has had any children at all.

How alone my body has been all these years.

꩜

Tomorrow the boys arrive. There will be the older ones whose faces have set into a mask of coping, their young bodies swaggering and shoving, their loud laughs belying the pain of their predicament. Here there is no parent to comfort or take pride in their achievements, no listening ear, no word of encouragement. Here it is dog eat dog, survival of the fittest, and the fittest learn quickly to fit in, they dare not look or behave differently, lest they be tortured and humiliated. The new boys will glance about, trying to understand their place in such a strange and unnatural world. Those who fail to read the code will have their noses painfully rubbed in their mistakes, like innocent puppies.

Please, God, let me ease their suffering. Let me be the steadfast light that shows these innocents the way to Your great goodness.

꩜

I knew it was she the moment I saw her. I was going downstairs yesterday afternoon to usher another batch of new boys and their parents to the sick bay, so that they could hand over any medication and notify me of chronic complaints. As I turned the corner of the stairway, I looked straight at her. She was illuminated amongst the throng in the entrance hall, like a painting by one of the old masters, for the afternoon sun shone through the lead-paned window above my head, directly onto her.

You were pointing her out to me, Lord.

She held her body in a stance which eerily evoked her father, despite her never having met him: somewhat tense, expectant, with the same broad brow. Her blunt chin, like his, was tilted slightly forward as she glanced around. I had a wild, mad thought that perhaps it was me she was looking for. At her elbow stood a boy with severely Brylcreemed hair, looking out at the rowdy scene of baggage and parents and chauffeurs and boys as though from behind ramparts; I noticed also that he pulled incessantly at the sleeves of his new blazer, which was too big for him. A hiatus opened, and it seemed a goodly while before I was able to move, or to think, or to act in any way. Her gaze (searching for what? What had she searched for in her thirty-eight years? What had she discovered?) flitted over my astonished face, then returned and found my eyes, her gaze settling upon and looking into mine, and I saw in that heavenly afternoon light that her eyes were brown, with a slightly down-turned shape, like my own.

A bolt ran through me; fearing that my life of pain was writ clear upon my features in a dark and terrible script, I turned and fled, fairly running up the stairs and back to my room, my heart in a panic, my mind sliding away.

For a good half hour I sat on my bed, my fingers nervously pleating the hem of my skirt, weeping and scolding myself for neglecting my duties. I had never thought beyond this point. What now, Lord? I do not wish to appear ungrateful, but am faced with the awful truth that one must indeed be very careful what one asks for, as one's prayers might well be answered.

What is one to say? Who is this woman, and how am I to speak to her? It is possible I am wrong, but what if I am right? I cannot let this opportunity You have provided slip through my fingers.

I found myself trembling, shaking even, as tears dripped onto my serge skirt. It was my old companion shame that had got me by the throat.

Outside in the corridor, I could hear the murmur of voices: parents, no doubt come to find me. And she probably among them, I imagined – the baby girl who now had an immutable name, a history, a life. The door still has no lock, for I am not allowed one. I would be found out, I feared; I would lose my job, and with it, the roof over my head.

A rap at the door. "Matron!" Mr Talbot, come to fire me. Terrified, I slid off the bed and onto my knees, the mattress squealing derisively, giving me away. Dear Lord, please save me, I prayed, as I wriggled awkwardly under the bed and lay wheezing amongst the dust motes as the door opened. How had I foreseen that he would dare to intrude into a lady's room? I lay there, blood pounding in my ears, horrified that my shoes might be visible, and trying to suppress the thin bagpipe sound emanating from my throat. I watched under the fringe of the counterpane as Mr Talbot's buffed shoes walked across the floor. A green light spilt onto the floor as he opened the door into the sick bay.

"Willoughby, have you seen Matron?" he snapped at Martin, who had arrived that morning by train with a fever.

"No, sir," came the timid reply. I realised: we were all afraid of this man with his tapered face, his plaited brow.

Instead of leaving my room, Mr Talbot's shoes turned, hesitated, then squeaked straight towards me. I braced myself for the lifting of the counterpane, for the lowered head, for the terrible moment of exposure and humiliation. The shoes stopped within inches of my nose. Through the deafening thumping of my blood, I heard him inspect objects on my bedside table. I was trapped, trapped, with my life on display to people who do not care for me. The tunnel opened, that ever-present chute ready to swallow me, blackness stuffing down my throat. Then the shoe turned, brushing my lips with the taste of polish and dirt as he set an item down and left again, closing the door behind him. I heard his murmured apologies to the waiting parents; then his brisk footsteps faded down the passage.

I lay labouring for air in this coffin-black place.

Look at you! Nothing but a lump of lard hiding from life. You're ridiculous! Get yourself up, this minute!

She whips me out of the dark, that voice, she keeps me going. I dragged myself out, bumping my knee on the iron bedstead, and reached for my mask, pumping relief into my lungs.

What a miserable mess confronted me in the mirror! Hastily, I splashed my eyes at the basin and dragged a brush through my disordered hair, then dusted myself off. Phyllis, stop being silly. Your imagination has run amok! It's true. I jump to conclusions with scant evidence. And look at the consequences! Late for my duties, with my eyes puffed and red! I squeezed drops into my eyes, and fixed a smile to my face. Then I stepped through the door into the sick bay.

Little Martin Willoughby's eyes widened. "Mr Talbot . . ."

"I know," I smiled. "How are you feeling now, Martin?"

"Much better, thank you, Matron."

"Then slip on your dressing gown and go and tell Mr Talbot I am found, and that I am busy with the parents."

He slid out of bed to do my bidding.

I went over to the door leading from the sick bay into the corridor, straightened my jacket, and made my entrance.

Five parents with their sons looked up with surprise from their chairs in the corridor, she being the first of them, immediately to my right.

"Come in," I welcomed her. "Sorry to have kept you."

She and the boy followed me into the procedure room, which doubles as an office and is where the folders with the boys' medical details are kept. I turned to her and offered my hand. "I am Matron Wilds," I said lightly, studying her face, which appeared hard to the point of brittleness. Had I been mistaken? There was no sign in her of Alan's kind smile, although her jaw-line was reminiscent of his. The initial strong impression might well have been a trick of the light in the hallway, or an errant flicker of my mind.

That moment – the first time I touched my child, if indeed it was her – I held out my hand, my heart leaping in my chest. She gripped it without much interest, then quickly dropped it. "Mrs Cunningham," she said, sitting on the edge of the seat in her tight skirt. She wound one stockinged leg around the other, placed her handbag on her lap and rummaged around in it. Producing a lipstick and compact, she applied another layer of bold red to her lips. "And this is Michael," she said, gesticulating vaguely in his direction with the scarlet tube.

"Welcome, Michael," I said. "I hope you will be happy here."

I opened the folder. "Mrs . . .?"

"Cunningham," she repeated irritably, leaning back and casting a critical eye around the room. "Susan Cunningham."

Paging through the file of the new standard six boys, I could not find his details.

"Oh, no," Susan explained, "Michael is in standard eight."

I was at a loss for words. This child was too small, too delicate. He would never survive here. But there he was, down for the standard eight dormitory in the north wing: Michael Kendrew Cunningham, date of birth 5 January 1940.

"And Mr Cunningham?" Most of the new boys were accompanied by both parents. Very often, the fathers had themselves attended the school.

"He didn't survive the war," she explained, in a matter-of-fact manner, looking at her watch. "It's all on the application form."

"I'm sorry," I offered. What does one say to this? Poor boy, most of his life without a father, now to live without a mother, too. He stood beside her, his face blank. His skin was soft, like a girl's. "Don't let the housemasters catch you with your hands in your pockets," I warned him kindly. He whipped them out, and I had a glimpse of his bitten nails.

"We are not from the Cape," Susan sighed, tucking a wisp of auburn hair under her smart little hat. "But my husband attended this school, and his grandfather thought it best . . ." She was telling me that none of this was her fault.

"The school has a good reputation," I assured her. What I wanted to say was how horrified I felt by how little he was, too small for this place, too innocent. "Any medical problems?" I continued.

"Asthma," she replied, then added firmly: "He's not to do sport."

Asthma. He has asthma.

I had to know. "Does it run in the family? Are you a sufferer? And your parents?"

She nodded. "I had asthma as a child. But I am fine now. He'll grow out of it."

"And your parents?" I insisted.

"They're fine," she snapped.

She doesn't know she is adopted. Or she refuses to reveal it. I applied my shaking hand to the task of writing this down. It is all in the blood, blood to blood, blood passed down, running down through the valleys of the generations. Before me sat my blood issue, spilt, almost lost. But she does not know it, and appeared to stare right through me.

Lord, my God, help me.

I raised my head. "I have asthma," I told her. "Don't you worry. He's in good hands." Not playing sport will mark the rest of his school life, every moment of his three years here. He will be despised for that, unable to prove himself in the physical world, already doomed to failure. He will most certainly be crushed by the large bully rugby players like Roger Granger, who rule the school.

I understand now what You have done, Lord. You have sent him to me so that I can protect him. My grandson, my darling boy, I will look after you, I promised him and myself. I will position myself between you and all danger. I wanted to write this down, to stamp and seal it.

"Look, I really do have to go now," she said, and stood up. I found myself shaking her hand again and mouthing pleasantries, and watching her straight back as she turned and left, walking through the door, returning to her life without me.

Susan! I wanted to call after you. I need you to know I am not a mere servant in this posh establishment. I am your mother.

You have left me your son. Michael. I like the name Michael.

But I dislike the name Susan, and I don't much like the person you have become. I called you Kitty those months you were inside me, all curled up and warm.

A stupid name, a childish name.

But that's what you were. Kitty, little Kitty.

Mummy said to me once when I was small and my cat gave birth to a litter: sometimes you have to give little kitties away.

Of course, it is all my own doing. I produced a child and had to give her away to strangers who, it appears from the way Susan has turned out, were totally unsuitable.

I cannot find my way out of darkness. Its stain remains on everything I touch. A watercolour I began a few weeks ago lies rolled up and discarded at the bottom of the cupboard. It is lifeless, any hint of light on the mountain drowned in brown. Rebecca West lies unopened on my bedside table.

There is pus beneath the surface, sewn in all those years ago. I can go on no longer, yet I must.

⟜

Mr Talbot spoke very well in his address to the boys at dinner last night. He told them the parable of the talents, explaining that if one does not develop and use one's talents, which are God-given, these gifts will be taken from one, and life will become very difficult. He urged the boys to apply themselves with diligence, whether on the sportsfield or in the classroom, or even in the dormitories, where they all have their duties to perform.

He warned them that if they did not apply themselves they could expect punishment, initially at school, but later from life itself, which would cast them aside. All of which, to my regret, is perfectly true. I hope Michael takes his words to heart.

All through Mr Talbot's address I kept slipping glances at the boy, who was sitting rather too far away for me to read his expression. He wasn't restless like some of the others, and appeared to be paying attention.

Perhaps any boy whose mother voluntarily gives her child up is, by that very fact, better off at boarding school. Perhaps there are values here that will stand him in good stead, living as he does without a father's guidance.

The sun pools light and warmth on my counterpane; outside, a bird sings joyfully for the Lord.

I have my duties for the day, starting with Martin Willoughby next door who is ready for discharge. Yet the cold hand of the devil stays my foot. I will wrench myself from his grasp and start again today.

Perhaps it is not too late to mend what has been broken.

⌒

I must stop this. I have wasted another of God's precious days waiting at my window, hoping for a glimpse of the boy.

Mr Leighton oversees the dormitory Michael is assigned to, so I have no opportunity there.

I could send for him, but on what pretext? What would I say? I am afraid I will put him off.

Until now I have thought of her as a golden-haired child, innocent and pure, even though she was conceived in sin. I have always assumed that the barren parents would have been kind and gentle to their little foundling, their gift from God. I did not expect that she would turn out to be a rude, hard woman who does not appear to appreciate her own child.

God has taken Michael away from her, and given him to me for safekeeping. He has looked into both our hearts, and has seen: I am the better mother.

Patience, Phyllis. You are a small part of God's great design. The wheel is finally turning.

My darling sister is coming to town for the opening of Parliament. She tells me she'll be driving in a cavalcade from Johannesburg, a cavalcade of women drivers who will stage protests and gather support, with their black sashes, in the towns they pass through. They are coming to Cape Town to try to persuade Parliament not to pass the Act that will disenfranchise coloured male voters. Phoebe actually believes she is that powerful.

Or perhaps not. Perhaps she is out for the ride, loving the spotlight. After all, these women are all over the newspapers. In one of the small dorps, they have even been attacked for their beliefs. They are heroines. And now Phoebe is one of them.

They arrive tomorrow, and plan to parade down Adderley Street before addressing a meeting at the Parade. I can just imagine it – Phoebe and the old mad prophet, pronouncing the End of the World.

One might well argue that it is indeed the end of the world when a grandmother abandons her duties assisting her daughter-in-law with her new baby in order to take part in public disturbances.

Should I tell her about Michael? She has always behaved as though she has no niece in the world. Perhaps she has put it so far out of her mind that she believes it never happened. All I know is, if she carries on and on about her own little grandchild, I might just shut her up with evidence of mine.

Grace is back. It is hard to tell whether she is perpetually down in the dumps, or whether she is merely inscrutable. She has put on weight in the holidays. Women tend to fall apart physically after an emotional upheaval. It happened to me too. Yet her face draws me. I still cannot see it as beautiful, but I do feel a certain fascination. I wonder whether I might paint her? Whether she would allow it?

I have decided that I won't go to see the arrival of the cavalcade. Though Phoebe has asked me to, I won't. I have a million things to complete around here since the boys have arrived. Some of us have real work to do.

I have never seen anything like it. Adderley Street was packed with people of all colours, jostling to get a view of the cars sporting banners showing where they had come from. Benoni, Springs, Pretoria, Graaff-Reinet, Port Elizabeth, East London, Pietermaritzburg, Durban, Johannesburg. To name just a few. One car had a large papiermâché book attached to a roof rack at an angle so that people could read its title: *The Constitution*. Draped across the book was a black sash.

I craned my neck, trying to see Phoebe, and to see whether she had driven down in one of Bryan's Mercedes's, but I could not get near the front of the crowd. As the cavalcade approached the Parade, I decided I had had enough, and caught the train home.

I feel shaken, somehow. I had no idea that this was so serious. Perhaps the government will sit up and take notice. Perhaps women can engage in public life, after all.

But I don't feel like seeing Phoebe. She is staying with an old friend of hers, Eleanor Hamilton, in Rondebosch. Phoebe and I were never much good for each other, and I don't suppose that will change now. I don't want her to see me living in this green room with two doors, even though it was her idea. I don't want her to see me at all.

⤳

I was in the art room this morning, washing down the windows, which were absolutely filthy, with Rory trying to persuade me that my time would be better spent painting. I replied that it is important to have an orderly and light workplace so as to concentrate and to work efficiently. Rory snorted at that, and called me down from the stepladder to show me photographs of the studios of two famous artists I have never heard of, a Mr Pollock and a Mr Bacon. I have never seen anything like it. I don't know how they get anything done. Their mothers must have had a terrible time with them.

He then read from the book, trying to distract me from my task. Personally, I think these artist types are merely out to shock. One of them said he likes throwing himself in the gutter, and that every artist wants to do so as part of the necessity of life. He claimed that if he hadn't turned to painting, he would have been a criminal!

Rory appeared taken with this point of view. He proposed that the comforts we enjoy, and indeed desire, can be quite deadening to an artist – and this from a man who has had a good education! I wanted to object to several aspects of his argument, and was trying to get my thoughts in order when Phoebe arrived, interrupting us. Full of gush and vigour, she exclaimed how exhausted she was, having participated in an all-night vigil at the parliament buildings. She reported that there were as many as four hundred women wearing black sashes standing around the building, trying to embarrass the government into not passing the Act. A waste of good black material, don't you think? I blurted out. Both she and Rory looked at me as though I was a worm that had just crawled out of their apple.

I could see what she was doing. Through this one story, she has managed to cast me in a lesser light for not having been there, and to impress Rory with her affectation of bravery. She practically turned her back on me, and focused on him, telling stories about how members of the Black Sash had been attacked during vigils in both the Transvaal and the Free State. An angry white man had spat in her friend's face, some women had had their sashes torn off, and in one shocking situation, a mother had given her daughter a rotten tomato to throw at a protester outside Parliament.

Rory was completely taken in. They immediately fell to, discussing politics over tea, ignoring me. Mortified, I excused myself, saying I had a headache, and went to sit in my room.

Everything Phoebe touches turns to gold. Everything my hand comes into contact with becomes dross.

How dare she? How dare she come to visit me, then spend the time beguiling that impressionable young man? And she is a married woman, at that.

Telling her about Susan and Michael is now completely out of the question. She is not a person one can trust with delicate information.

When she eventually came upstairs to my room, I pretended I wasn't there, so she gave up knocking. I sat still and waited until long after the clip-clip of her high heels on the corridor floor had faded away.

She could, after all, have tried the door and found it open. So, clearly, she didn't really want to see me at all.

⤙

The headline today: "The South African Act Amendment Act has been passed". I am pleased that, for once, Phoebe has not got her way.

⤙

Michael is, as I suspected, a loner, occasionally hanging around the periphery of a group on the hall steps, but mostly he is by himself, reading in the library, or walking alone in the corridor. He is in the north-wing upstairs dormitory, and shares a cubicle with Stephen Parsons. Stephen had been in the sick bay with measles last year, one of the few boys I have got to know through illness or injury. Even the tough chaps are vulnerable when set apart from the fortification of their group, and out of uniform. Illness in particular seems to divest them of their armour of bravura, underneath which hides a small boy who desperately misses his mother.

There are a few who visit me after a sojourn in the sick bay, who remember my care, yet they are careful not to be seen doing so. Stephen is one of them, Adrian Flower another. They are the bullied ones, those looking for a brief respite. I make them tea, and offer them a biscuit. Adrian Flower shyly brings me poems he has written or a book he is reading, and Stephen Parsons will tell me about his dog, Flame, so far away at home in Southern Rhodesia, or show me a sketch he has made of a strelitzia.

I want to ask Stephen about Michael, but it would seem strange, strained. I am ashamed to say it has occurred to me to pray for Michael to get sick. It was an idle thought, Lord, forgive me. You will surely bring him to me in Your own good time.

~

Try as I might, I cannot get that ridiculous idea out of my head – the notion that painting, as an activity, can prevent a man from becoming a criminal! It is obvious that those who have profitable employment will not turn to crime, and this artist – Mr Francis Bacon, I think it is – much as he might claim to want to be in the gutter, has apparently earned very well from his work, and has no need to steal. Yet Rory snorted at my explanation, saying that criminal behaviour is also found amongst the wealthy, whose means of acquiring wealth is often enough criminal. I had to laugh at this, for Mummy would have agreed with him on this opinion, though on no other!

He then spoilt our conversation altogether by turning to politics again, going on about the Nationalist government and their criminal laws, so I made my excuses. Now I sit alone at my table with my questions unanswered. Not that I can even frame it into a question, this commotion that goes on inside me. And if I do not have a question clearly formulated, how can anyone give me an answer?

I am not a criminal in that I am a Christian, and make an effort to abide by Christ's decrees and do my Christian duty. But this Mr Bacon says he is not a criminal *because* he is a painter!

I just cannot get to the question.

⌒

Dear Lord, what to do? I could put those boys over my knees and give them all a good hiding with my hairbrush! Yesterday I glanced out of the sick bay window overlooking a small quad that is usually deserted, to see a circle of boys grouped around someone smaller. They were pushing the poor thing from one to another, and, judging from the sniggers, taunting him as well. I opened the sash window and shouted for them to stop. They all turned abruptly away and left, hands in pockets and heads down, the cowards, and the small boy darted off in the opposite direction. It all happened too fast for me to be able to identify any of the boys, but I am concerned that the little one was Michael.

Michael is the smallest in his class. I have a clear view of this during cadets. He has obviously not done drill before and is hopelessly out of sync. Mr Paine, or Captain Paine, as he is known on the parade ground, is impatient with the poor thing. Susan said he should do no exercise; perhaps we can get him out of cadets on those grounds.

I wanted to approach him this evening, to try to strike up a conversation, and also to winkle out of him whether he was indeed the boy I'd seen being bullied. He was sitting by himself on the hall steps with a book open on his lap, apparently memorising something, perhaps a poem, I imagined. He was concentrating so deeply that I decided to wait for him to finish, and took the time to study him. Despite his freckles and the tendency to bite his nails, he is a pleasant-looking boy, his expession more animated because of the content of what he was committing to memory. I was surprised to discover a shyness in myself about approaching him, even a wariness. So much of my history is concentrated in this child.

I waited too long – before I could decide to join him, the prep bell went, summoning both him and me to our duties. On reflection, I am very glad he is in standard eight, and will therefore never witness my regular humiliation during standard seven prep.

He probably has better things to do than converse with someone who must appear to him to be an old lady. Fifty-four seems young if you are seventy, but dreadfully old if you are only fifteen.

It has occurred to me to contact Alan. I have even looked up the telephone number of the Zoology Department and have it in my purse. But what to say?

I want to tell him: I have found her, and she has a beautiful son. It couldn't have been so wrong, then, what we did, who we were. I want to ask him, do you even remember me? Have you ever once wondered what became of me? Have you ever lain awake at night filled with a desperate longing?

These are stupid fancies. Alan would be embarrassed by me now; he has forgotten that holiday altogether. He has had many other far more wonderful holidays since then, whereas I have treasured that one as my single golden experience of life.

⌒

Mr Talbot has sent a message that he wants to see me in his office tomorrow. I do not know what to think, and it has gone straight to my chest. He has found me out, but in connection with what? Prep continues to be a nightmare, with practical jokes and passed notes. I have attempted to point out to the boys that their parents are paying a fortune for their education, and that they had better appreciate it. I nearly added "or else". Or else what? Or else I get hauled into Mr Talbot's office.

There are, of course, other reasons he might want to see me – my chest, for example – but that has been much better of late, except when these upsets come along. And then there is that terrible matter of Andrew Brannaghan's medication that I gave to Phil Parrish by mistake, but thank goodness Phil was unaffected by it. It makes one wonder what they put into these preparations, that anyone can take a dose willy-nilly.

Perhaps someone has told him that I have a bottle of sherry in my cupboard – kept only for emergencies, mind you.

Or someone saw me that time at the standard seven dormitory window, watching those boys. Please, God, anything but that.

Or could the housemaster somehow have uncovered my past? That would surely be the worst. Were he to find out about Susan, I would certainly be expelled. Dismissed, rather. Fired. With no good reference.

Lit from behind by the setting sun, the mountain poses with authority and grandeur in the frame of the window. Should I be found out and lose my job, Phoebe would have to have me, and I would need to move to Johannesburg and lose even this.

I would rather hang myself.

No good, no good, no good will come of me! Who can I turn to? Father, forgive me, I have sinned, and am lost. You are the Good Shepherd, yet there will come a time when even You will not be able to find me in these darkest of nights. There are certain things that are beyond help, beyond hope. Even if Father Nichols had been a good replacement for Father Evans, as I had hoped, or if I had – oh, I talk around myself, I fret and scribble, but these are mere words and phrases, they are ink on paper, they bear no relation to the real horror of life.

This afternoon Mr Talbot closed the door of his study quietly, showed me a chair, and sat down next to me rather than at his usual place behind the desk. He linked his hands in front of him and placed his elbows on the arm rests, leaning forward on them, so that his long face appeared even longer, and threads of veins on the bulb of his nose became suddenly apparent. His liver-brown eyes stared at me. His mouth opened, but before he could fire me, I blurted out that I hoped he had had a good trip to America. This was a rather stupid thing to say because, of course, Mrs Talbot had already informed us all at table how wonderful their vacation was. He nodded, brushing a hand across his temple as though brushing away all thought of America. "My wife has come back with several lovely handbags," he said, with a smile that could only be described as sardonic.

Why was he telling me about his wife's handbags? He then leaned back and surveyed me down the length of his nose. "How are things with you, Matron? May I call you Phyllis? I like to catch up with my staff every now and then, and you have been with us," he checked the file lying open on his desk, "almost a year."

I nodded, not knowing what was expected of me. Then, under

pressure from the silence that followed, while Mr Talbot stared at my reddening face, I heard myself mumble how happy I was to be working at such a reputable establishment.

He nodded without enthusiasm, then drew in a breath and looked up at a point above my head, pressing his fingertips together and preparing to speak. "It appears, Phyllis, that I have high blood pressure." He scanned my face for a response, which I struggled to summon to my frozen features. "Ian Cudgel has prescribed medication that I must take every day, like some old man." He smiled wryly. "There was a time when I was an athlete of note. Does that surprise you? High blood pressure runs in the family, so I am not all that surprised, but nevertheless, it has made me aware, let me say, of my mortality. Twenty-six years ago I witnessed my father die of a stroke. Have you ever seen anyone die? Anyone close to you? Do you ever think about mortality, Phyllis? I believe you are a religious woman."

The full focus of his gaze fell on me, and I was required to express a view, to comfort, to encourage. There was not enough air in the room. Was this a test? Did he somehow know that I was not with my mother when she died? It still troubles my conscience.

I prayed that my words were the ones he wanted to hear: "Oh, yes, Mr Talbot. I believe in Jesus as our Saviour, and in the hereafter."

"Yes, yes, but beyond that, Phyllis. You have asthma, I have high blood pressure. These are illnesses that can be treated, but that can also carry one off," he snapped his fingers, "just like that."

What was he asking me? "Father Nichols is probably the best person . . . to talk to about . . . or Doctor Cudgel . . ."

Mr Talbot whisked the suggestion away with a flick of his hand.

"Oh, Ian Cudgel and Father Nichols have their stock phrases. I am looking for a real conversation. I thought, looking at you the other day at table, that perhaps there was an intelligence we had underestimated." I felt myself rise to his flattery. To think that this important man had noticed me!

The housemaster cocked an eyebrow at me. "I see you are reading *Lady Chatterley's Lover*."

I felt I had been winded. He has been into my room. Again. Seeing my expression, Mr Talbot hastily explained: "I was looking for you yesterday."

My blood turned to fire, searing my cheeks. I am certain I had hidden the book away beneath my underwear in my bedside drawer. It is not a book I would leave lying around. But yesterday, on returning to my room after prep, I was horrified to find it lying on top of the pedestal, in broad daylight.

"A friend . . . lent it to me," I blurted. "It is not a book I would usually . . . " I knew I should not have taken it from Judy, but my curiosity had got the better of me – my usual undoing. Stupid, stupid girl.

He shrugged off my protestations. "You do know, that book could get you removed from your position." He paused to give his utterance emphasis, then continued: "Personally, I suspect that we all have secret lives. As long as they remain secret, they can do no harm."

He was staring at me with his flecked eyes, noting my every reaction. His lips thinned with the effort of smiling. He extended his hands, palms outwards, looking, for one confusing moment, like Jesus summoning the little children. "Come and sit on my lap."

I found myself at the door, with my hand on the doorknob. "I really must go," I said, or some such thing, something about giving the boys their medication.

"Matron!" he called after me as I fled down the passage. I hesitated, and turned to see him at his office door, a commanding man, a man who could not be ignored. "I'll see you tomorrow." He tapped his arm above the elbow. "Blood pressure check."

～

Just below the play of light on the surface, there are shadows and secrets. Mr Talbot says we all have them. Could this be so? Throughout dinner, I was unable to look at Mr Talbot, though I did glance several times at Mrs Talbot's face, and realised with shock that I know something about her husband which she does not.

I am terrified he has found this journal and knows my innermost thoughts. It is secured under my mattress – I do not know whether he would think to look there. Why do I risk this yet again? One would expect me to have learnt my lesson as a girl after Mummy had found my journal. I remember believing at the time that if Mummy hadn't read about my love for Alan and marched me off to Doctor Riley, he would not have discovered I was pregnant and I therefore would not have had a baby.

I should give this up and burn it. Yet I am afraid that if I do so, I will forget entirely who I am.

He arrived in the procedure room today, sat in a chair and rolled up his sleeve, exposing a rather pale and stringy upper arm. The sick bay has a Baumanometer for Doctor Cudgel's use, but I did not get that far in my nurse's training, which I hurriedly explained, grateful for this fact and for the two boys practically within earshot in the sick bay. He pulled his sleeve down again, saying that he would instruct the doctor to teach me. He sat staring at me, then asked me what I thought of the book.

What book? I asked, my face burning.

You know, he said.

I shook my head, for in truth I have not yet opened it.

Just underneath that pale skin of his arm lie long tubes filled with blood. Just underneath the skin it is dark and hot; life pulses, wanton and violent.

He touched my shoulder as he left, briefly clamping it. It felt like the touch of death. *What kind of woman has that kind of book in her possession?* Of course he has an idea about who I am now, I don't blame him, but I am mortified to think of it.

My body is a-jangle, alert for every step that falls outside my door, lest he try to have his way. My room, this one place which I try to claim as a sanctuary, has been violated.

I have given the troublesome book back to Judy without reading it, for which she laughed at me, but I cannot tell her the truth of what has happened. I cannot tell her that the world turns on Satan's fork, that the pure skin of the world has been pierced by malevolence.

⌒

My opportunity arrived in a terrible way. This is how our darkest prayers are answered. Michael arrived in the sick bay with a swollen finger and red eyes. He told me he had hurt himself trying to catch a cricket ball, but I noticed he had a swelling on his temple as well, and that he was limping. I was immediately concerned, and sat him down with a cup of tea and a biscuit, which these ravenous boys always enjoy. Then I asked him to tell me what was really going on. Since the Flower and Cameron episodes, I usually refrain from probing too deeply. How am I to protect any of them when I cannot protect myself?

Stupid girl.

He insisted that the ball had also hit his temple as he tried to catch it, but I could see fear furtive in his restless eyes. I examined the finger, and did not think it broken, so I bandaged it up and told him that if it was still sore in the morning, he should present to Doctor Cudgel. I then offered another biscuit to delay him, and as he wolfed it down, I asked him a little about himself and his love of books. It turns out that he has just read all of the Swallows and Amazons series, which I had also enjoyed as a girl. Your grandfather also loved the outdoors, I wanted to tell him, and noticed how small the lobes of his ears are, just like Alan's. Instead, I told him of a time when I was a girl and had a friend who had a canoe, and how we explored Sandvlei before there were any houses there, and built a fire on the small island in the middle, baking potatoes, and bananas with chocolate, and how we pretended we were castaways, living happily out of reach of rules and expectations.

Of course, I added, we were trying to live inside a fairy story, but even in fairy stories bad things happen.

At this his lower lip began to quiver, but he controlled it by raising his teacup to his mouth. I know someone has been hurting you,

I told him. If you ever want to tell me about it, we can see if there is something we can do. Besides, I know from experience that terrible things can happen to a person, and if you tell someone who sympathises, and so share the burden, it will feel better. He glanced at me, and his eyes were two wells of pain. I could see that he was contemplating something, that words were hovering at his lip, when out in the corridor the infernal dinner bell rang. He jumped up and gave a funny half-bow to thank me, and fled.

I am tired, but I do not want to go to bed. What on earth am I to do about this, or about anything? I have never managed to do enough for my own flesh and blood.

The doors of this room do not lock, and I have taken to jamming my chair and another from the hall under the doorknobs of the two doors. I do not know whether this will be of any use should someone try to open a door in the night.

Beneath the surface of the beautiful school buildings, small beings lie curled up in the sheath of their own individual terror. My bed seethes with nightmares, my pillow holds my head like an offering on an altar to devilish ends.

These are mad notions, which I must put out of my mind. Things could be a lot worse. I must keep my head.

Tomorrow will be better, Lord, with You to guide and help us. Fairy tales, after all, do have happy endings. Please, God, help Michael and me through this dark wood.

⌐

Mummy died in the night. She had a habit of ringing her bell just as I was dropping off, so that I would have to drag myself up only to discover that all she wanted was the glass of water that was right next to her on the bedside table. I understood. She was lonely, that was all, and terrified of death, so I would sit beside her and stroke her hand until she fell back into sleep. Sometimes I was so tired I would get into bed and doze off beside her, and at times I'd wake to the cloying wetness of her urine seeping over the rubber bed sheet.

That night I could not rouse myself from my bed. Mummy had called me *stupid* when I brought her a hot-water bottle, saying she'd burn herself, it was so hot, and did I want to kill her? I had snapped back, close to breaking point, trying so hard, and it was never, never good enough, and I was tired, so tired. Sweet Jesus, I could never be as good as You, and Mummy never forgave me for that. So when her bell tinkled furiously at two in the morning, I put a pillow over my head. You punished me on that night and forever more, for my selfishness will always be with me, that I let a defenceless, sick, bed-ridden old woman – no, not any old woman, *my mother* – die alone.

I am a dreadful child.

In the morning her body was already cold. The look on her face will haunt me forever. It was a look of utter forsakenness.

I failed you, Mummy. Not once, but many times. Forgive me, I did not know what I was doing.

⸻

Michael arrived in the sick bay this afternoon, complaining of a headache and a tummy ache. I took his temperature and his pulse, both of which were normal. Nevertheless, I told him to get into his pyjamas, then popped him into bed and gave him an aspirin. If he were faking illness, there was good reason, I surmised. And good reason to be with me. I brought him tea and the last of the biscuits, which were already a bit stale, but that did not seem to bother him.

It's not too long before the Easter vacation, I consoled him, thinking he was homesick. You'll be looking forward to going home then.

He looked away through the window. My mother can't have me home, he said. I'm to stay here. I was shocked. The only boys who stayed at school for the short holidays were those who came from faraway places like Northern Rhodesia, and who were not popular enough to be invited home by friends. But Michael was from Johannesburg, a mere two days by train. Why wouldn't he be going home for the ten-day vacation?

I eventually got it out of him. Susan is to have a procedure in hospital – Michael was not at all sure what for. Initially I was worried, but after a while I thought it sounded like an excuse – why does it have to be in the boy's holiday?

I couldn't bear the expression on Michael's face; it was as though he had pulled down a shutter. Underneath, there was presumably so much torment that he could not let it show.

Never mind, I told him. I'll also be here for the holidays. We'll find some nice things to do together. He looked at me in disbelief, but had the grace to nod.

If only I could keep you here and safe in your bed. I would tend you and care for you. I would find the key and lock the door. Together, we would be safe from all intruders, from everyone who wishes us harm. I will knit for you and bring you treats, and dress your wounds and put a poultice on your bruises. I will not let you lift a finger. Darling boy, I could weep for fear and happiness that I have found you.

He is there now, still in the bed, alone in the sick bay, for I discharged Brian Selby whom, I thought, was malingering.

The kettle is on for cocoa, and fortunately I have two marshmallows left over from my over-indulgence yesterday. If I spoil him, he may return again. I want him to know that here, he will always find solace.

He is asleep next door. I sat with him, stroking his arm to help him drop off. He opened his clear eyes and said how nice it was, my touch. After he had fallen asleep, I continued to sit and watch him for a long time. His is the face of innocence, with long lashes curving from the vulnerable blueish edge of his eyelids, with hair just darkening at the corners of his mouth, with soft lips slightly parted, revealing perfect teeth.

I wanted to kiss him good night, to let my lips brush his so gently he might think it a dream, so that he might feel safe in a world that loves him, a world that will never hurt nor forsake him. I wanted to get into his bed and take him in my arms, and let his head fall against my breast and hold him close and feel his warm breath on my skin. My hand trembled, longing just to touch his cheek, but I was too afraid I would wake him.

Instead, I lay my head in my hands and let quiet tears drip between my fingers for everything that has happened, and because my great error means that he will always be out of reach, and can never come to know who I am and how much I love him.

I should write to Susan, and tell her what has happened to Michael, or at least what I think has happened, for he has not yet admitted to being bullied.

No, I should encourage him to tell her himself.

But then she might take him out of the school, and they will both be lost to me forever!

What if it is not a mere minor procedure, and she dies? Again, I will lose them both. This treasure is connected to me by a fragile and tenuous thread.

It is so very difficult to get to the truth of things, so that one might prepare oneself for the worst.

~

I was just giving Michael breakfast in bed – the regulation post toasties into which I had sliced one of my own bananas, and scrambled egg on toast – when Mr Talbot opened the door.

"Get up, Cunningham," he ordered.

"He has a bad tummy, Mr Talbot," I exclaimed, forgetting myself.

He glared at me, and I understood: he was going to make my life hell. Out of his pocket he pulled a note, which he thrust at me. "Hurry up, Cunningham! If you are late for class you will stay in for detention for the rest of the week."

The poor creature rushed off down the corridor to his dormitory without a backward glance either at me or his breakfast.

The note was from Mr Wickham, the cricket coach, and addressed to Mr Talbot. He said he thought Michael was malingering. "But he is not supposed to play cricket," I protested, not knowing where I got the courage, but feeling as though my very soul was at stake. "He is asthmatic, and his mother . . . "

"We know that, Matron. It is for that very reason Cunningham has been put in charge of the equipment, which is a responsible task, one which he should not shirk."

"But his tummy . . ."

"You are too soft in some arenas, and too hard in others. Not the qualities we are looking for in a matron." His eyes glittered like crushed glass. "Mr Wickham has excellent judgment. We are already bending over backwards to accommodate an unsuitable boy in a school known for its sporting excellence. I will inform Cunningham that if he thinks he is ill, he can report to Doctor Cudgel tomorrow, who has years of experience with malingering boys."

He turned to go. I could not bear it, that a boy I felt sure was being bullied would now also get into trouble with the authorities. "Mr Talbot!" He swung round. "I have reason to believe –" But I could not continue under the full glare of his gaze.

"What, Matron?" He looked at his watch.

"I . . ." Stupid girl. You have, as usual, misjudged the situation. "Perhaps . . . I have misjudged the situation, sir. I apologise."

Mr Talbot nodded, satisfied, and left.

I am still shaking from the encounter, buffeted by contradictory winds. What is the truth, Lord? Sloth is a sin, and perhaps . . . His cereal turns mushy and the egg congeals on the table next to me.

Perhaps I will paint it: a still life of the abandoned breakfast of an abandoned boy.

⤴

Rory had the standard eight pupils out in the sunshine with sketch-books yesterday. I was on my way back from the laundry when I saw them sitting and drawing under the oaks next to the tennis court, with my dear Michael amongst them. Rory spotted me, and called me over, inviting me to join the class. Imagine that! Of course, I refused. His instruction to the boys was most peculiar. He told them to look in the gardens for an object that they liked, as well as one that they didn't like, and to draw these in their natural setting.

Why on earth would one want to draw something one does not like? I was inordinately annoyed by this, yet this afternoon on my walk around the grounds, I found my eye wandering to various things with an unusual kind of attention, or curiosity: what did I like, or dislike, and why? It is surely true that God has made all things, and yet some objects appear to have the devil in them.

Samuel was raking the gravel path, and the cleared, neat path was most pleasing to the eye, whereas the section still strewn with leaves, in the haphazard way nature arranges things, was annoyingly untidy. It makes one wonder: God creates things in a certain way, and then men tidy them up. What does this say about Your aesthetics, Lord? Please forgive me – I do not mean to be rude.

Also, I have discovered that I prefer symmetrical pine cones to ones that are lopsided or damaged in some way. It seems obvious to me why this is so. Those with symmetry or fullness represent life as it should be lived, whereas those that have grown askew are deficient, or defective, and those that are decaying or damaged cannot fulfil the purpose for which God created them.

But then, I am ashamed of this thought when I think of Mummy, who surely had her place in God's Kingdom. Father Evans, who knew her well, assured us of this at the funeral. And then, what of Grace, whom I can hear wasting water again as she cleans the bathroom. What is God's purpose for someone like her?

She has a little cough that worries me; perhaps she has picked up whatever it is that her child died of, and should not be working in a sick bay, or even in a school full of healthy boys. Perhaps it is TB, although I have heard that TB causes weight loss, and Grace has put on weight. I should caution her about the puddings here – they do tempt one to go for a second helping.

I shall tell her to present to Doctor Cudgel tomorrow. He will know what to do.

Looking at her through the door into the sick bay as she stands on a chair to hang the freshly washed curtains, with the afternoon light slanting onto her features, I see that she really does have an extraordinary face. And even though she has put on weight, her body has a certain . . . grace – despite the episode with the vase, and the way she handles a broom. I wonder what she looks like naked.

My! One's thoughts do run away with one!

Of *course* people prefer to look at the things that are pleasing to look at, so why should it be different when it comes to drawing them? But then I think of that girl painted by Mr Soutine, whose portrait I have gone back to again and again, in the catalogue in the art room. Her face is not beautiful, and it distresses me to look at her, and yet she will not leave me alone. What perversity is that? And why did Mr Soutine choose to paint her? He no doubt had access to many beautiful women who would gladly have offered themselves as subjects. Yet he chose this peasant girl, who was stupid enough to take her clothes off for him.

Is it true what Rory says of the great painters, that they had intimate relations with their models? Could this girl have turned her doe eyes to his, and allowed him to place his hand, stained with red paint, upon her breast, feeling the tip of her nipple ignite the centre of his palm? Is it possible that she could have pulled him to her, or that he forced himself upon her, drawn by the promise concealed between her thighs?

If a woman takes off her clothes, does it not indicate that she is available?

Mr Soutine, you went on to greatness. What happened to this girl, this piece of nothing, this anonymous person who was incapable of being anything other than herself, shown, full blown, in the ruddy innocence of that plain face?

I will ask Michael to show me his sketchbook so that I can see what he likes and dislikes. It might be a door that reveals something of who he is. Perhaps, during the vacation, we can sit and draw together. It is now only two weeks away. What does one do with a fifteen-year-old? This is my chance to forge a bond with him, yet I am afraid he will be bored by me.

There are times I am bored by myself.

⌒

Mr Talbot, thank God, is ignoring me. Surely if he were to fire me for being in possession of a banned book, he would have done so already? When Ursula came for tea on Saturday, I wanted to tell her what happened, but I know how her mouth flies open at the slightest provocation, and I was afraid that word might get out.

I am stupid enough to think that my version of the incident in Mr Talbot's office would be believed.

What, exactly, did happen? Perhaps I'd imagined it, and he was merely trying to be friendly. What do I know of men?

Now he is not friendly at all, and will not even look at me at table. This feels almost as bad as his attempt at friendship, and my tummy gets into such a knot that I can hardly eat. Ursula would say that this is a good thing, that nervous energy keeps one's figure trim. Judging by her own figure, Ursula is a nervous wreck.

George's wife has finally left him, so the whole situation is in disarray. George keeps weeping into Ursula's neck and ruining her hairdo, and suddenly she's not so sure she wants to marry him after all.

It is perhaps a good thing I never married, with all the difficulties involved. Besides, God has obviously put me here on earth for a purpose other than having children and making a husband happy.

If only I could find out exactly what that purpose is.

⌒

It is a year today that Mummy died. I can hear her calling me reproachfully from the Maitland cemetery to come and visit her. I haven't been there for eleven months. It necessitates two trips by train and a long walk to reach her, not that that is any excuse. I must go today, yet I rail sinfully against this. While she was alive she made my life hell. I don't see why she should continue to do this after death.

Yesterday, on my walk around the grounds, I found a small bird's nest that had fallen out of a syringa tree. It was lined with downy feathers, and inside it was a broken egg filled with a black substance, probably an unborn chick gone bad. It has no smell, and is starting to unravel, so it must be an old abandoned nest. It is untidy and broken and pointless, somehow, the life within it subverted, failed, turned to dross. Yet it was home at one time, and although I do not like it, something made me notice it, then come back and examine it, and then carry it to my room. It sits on the windowsill now as I write, and although it is only fit for the compost heap, and is far from beautiful, and crudely made, I find my eye wandering back to it time and again.

A letter from Phoebe tells me they are moving to Cape Town as Bryan has taken up a position as superintendent at Somerset Hospital. The move is a bit late, now that Mummy's dead. And I don't know how she can bear to leave her grandchild, but then, she never was much of a mothering type, despite the gift of her three sons.

There is an unfairness that pervades everything.

One should feel glad about the proximity of siblings, shouldn't one? Yet I feel a long shadow coming over me – the failed sister.

Not that I am likely to see much of her, what with her busy life. I wonder what she will get up to next, seeing that the Black Organisation, or whatever it is called, failed at everything except making fools of themselves.

The school choir is practising in the hall; I can hear them from here. Their voices soar on the air twice a week, bringing me solace. I am familiar with the song they are learning:

Oh, for the wings, for the wings of a dove!
Far away, far away would I rove!
In the wilderness build me a nest,
And remain there forever at rest.

Beauty is a good thing to weep over, otherwise why would the good Lord have given us tear ducts? I am filled with a fervour, and will get out the pastels I treated myself to last week. I don't know what came over me in Mr Mandelstein's art shop, for I don't know much about pastels and I could barely afford them, but one must try – and then try to survive the consequences.

I will visit Mummy next weekend. Today, though, I must draw.

Please, Lord, help me, I do not know what I am doing.

⌒

Doctor Cudgel says that Grace is pregnant. Dear Lord, oh please, God, I pray that You have not answered my prayer inappropriately! I must find out if she has a husband. I don't know why my mind immediately assumes the worst.

To my satisfaction, the doctor has given her some treatment for her cough, and has assigned her to the laundry until she is better. On her return I will talk to her, and extract the truth.

I must be silly in the head! What would I do with the truth? Phone

Richard? Or his parents? This is none of my business, and I must put it out of my mind.

Elizabeth is working in Grace's place. I must say, I find her easier to have around, for she has a sunny demeanour, and is easy to engage with. I came in today to find her with the radio tuned to an African station which was playing some of their music, and with Graham Fancourt out of bed in his pyjamas. She was teaching him an African dance!

I was a bit taken aback at first, and concerned about the effects of vigorous movement on my patient's sinuses, but they were having such a good time I had to relent. They invited me to join in, but I wasn't going to make a fool of myself, despite my flirtation with Elvis Presley. Elizabeth is about my age, but astonishingly agile. My knees could never stand the strain of what she gets up to. I know I shouldn't allow it, I am looking for trouble, but what can only be described as her joie de vivre is infectious, and I found that my foot was tapping. However, I closed the curtains as a precaution. I don't know what the authorities would think – that the sick bay is turning into an amusement hall?

I wondered who she goes home to, and asked her after I had sent Graham off to have a bath, since he was sweating so much from the exertions. It turns out that the garden boy, Samuel, is her husband! I am pleased for Elizabeth, for he is courteous and helpful, and never smells of drink. She has two daughters and a son, and four grandchildren. What a full life. I quite envy her.

Now, that was a strange thing to think.

I should reply to Phoebe's letter, but what shall I say? I'll inquire whether they plan to purchase a home near the hospital. Fortunately, Somerset Hospital is reasonably far away. I would not care to have Phoebe living on my doorstep.

～

Last night I was woken by a knock on the corridor door, and lay for a while terrified at the possibilities, hoping that I had dreamt it. But it was repeated, more insistently, so I wrapped my dressing gown around me, and called out to establish who was there. It was Michael, complaining of a tummy ache again, saying he could not sleep, and did I have something for him.

I could have wept with gratitude and relief, and sat him down for a cup of cocoa, hoping he had come to confide in me. But he downed the tablet and the cocoa without saying anything more.

"Do you have grandmothers?" I asked, hoping to detain him a while. He nodded, and I felt the swell of envy.

"They must be glad to have you," I persisted.

He shrugged. His paternal grandmother is deaf and almost blind and has six children and seventeen grandchildren, and her only real interest is her two sons who were killed in the war – one of them being Michael's father. His maternal grandmother, the woman Susan thinks is her mother, also lives in Johannesburg, but they don't see much of her.

"Why not?" I dared ask him. I needed to know why this woman, who was so desperate for a child that she took on mine, now does not bother to see her.

"They don't agree," said Michael, but did not elaborate. My poor daughter, abandoned by both her mothers. It is no wonder she presents such a hard exterior.

But there is room for me, if Michael will have me. There is a chink, but I must tread carefully, so as not to frighten him away. Just as I treat the wagtail that feeds at my windowsill.

"What was your father like?" I asked him.

He shrugged again. "I was a baby when he died."

Of course. Fatherless boy.

I wonder whether Rory might be some kind of mentor, if Michael shows some interest in painting. We could sketch together in the garden during the holiday. We could watch the birds.

Birds? Since when do boys like watching birds? What is it that boys like to do? I will ask Rory. He will surely know.

Beware, Phyllis. Your thoughts are overtaking you.

He has told me all, and I feel my fury billow at my impotence. How dare they! Michael arrived at the sick bay this afternoon with a split lip that needed stitches. He initially reported that he had walked into a door, and stuck to this story during Doctor Cudgel's questioning. But I got it out of him after the doctor had left. They'd put him in an equipment bag and pulled tight the drawstring, and kicked him around, like a ball! This, the cricket team says, is to "toughen him up". My poor child! What will become of us?

He has bruises on his back and forearms too; no wonder he feigned illness last week rather than go back to the cricket ground.

I am outraged, but I know there is no point in going to the authorities. Christopher Carey got beaten by a master in another house last week for reporting a bullying incident. The master maintained he was lying.

Nevertheless, I found myself saying to Michael: "Why don't you report this to the coach?"

He looked at me, terror widening his eyes. "You must never tell," he demanded earnestly. "It is one of the first things they teach you here. Please, promise me you will not tell."

"You told me," I pointed out.

Almost weeping, he replied, "I thought I could trust you."

"Trust me to do what? Collude with the people who are hurting you?"

"You don't understand!" he said, beside himself.

But I do. I do. I understand that this is the devil, tossing us on the horns of an impossible dilemma.

⌣

The boys leave tomorrow. I have found out, and not from Michael, that he is to stay with Harry Slater, of all people, on his parents' farm in Elgin. Harry's father is some distant relative.

Why have You done this, Lord? At every turn, my best intentions are thwarted. Every day I must lever my bones out of bed to do a bidding other than my own. Have I not served You well? Does reward only manifest in heaven?

You tease me, Lord, putting this opportunity in my path, then snatching it away. I am a pathetic plaything in Your hand.

The vacation looms dreadfully. How will I fill the time? Only two boys are staying: Stephen Parsons, who is sweet enough, and a new boy, Douglas Monk, whom I don't know at all. I doubt that either will be ill or bored enough to seek my company.

The mountain stands, secure and bold, while we humans come and go, puffed up with our own importance, or defeated in the knowledge that we are as chaff before the wind. My repeated efforts to paint the mountain are ridiculous. It is an arrogance to think one can convincingly translate a throne of God into a few colours smeared on paper. The mountain does not need me to do this, and neither does God. It will endure long after my feeble efforts have disintegrated, scattered with dust and rubbish on a rubbish heap somewhere.

I can't help but feel deeply upset that Michael did not inform me of his plans, and this after I'd held out my hand to him.

Rory is incorrigible! He is working in oils from photographs he'd taken of carcasses at the butchery – on canvasses as tall as I am. He is here every day while the children are away, immersed in the abattoir of his creations. I must say that his efforts are not to my taste, they are becoming more and more – what shall I say? – violent, I suppose. Less and less attractive. I cannot imagine anyone wanting to hang these paintings on their walls. It's a waste of good paint and canvas, if you ask me. And yet he has enough faith in his own preoccupation to have booked a space at the Metropolitan Gallery in town, an exercise that will surely cost him a pretty penny.

He commented this evening, under the influence of the sherry we have taken to sharing as the autumn light deepens and a winter chill begins to cloud the breath, that for the first time, he feels free. This, while concocting images that to me resemble bondage and death!

"What do you mean?" I asked him.

He said he was afraid to talk about it, it was so ephemeral. Talking about it might break the spell. I don't believe in spells, so I pushed him further. "I cannot see any difference in you from the outside," I challenged him. "We are all still busy with the same old round, me in the sick bay, you with teaching and your paintings. The only real freedom," I ventured, "is through Jesus Christ Our Lord."

He stared at me. "From what I remember of Sunday school," he retorted, "Jesus encapsulated the idea of freedom brought about through bondage and death."

I felt thoroughly annoyed, as though he was deliberately twisting my words, but he seemed unaware of my disapproval, and continued, quite taken by his analogy. "That's it!" he said, and gestured at the canvasses stacked around the room, all of which dripped flesh and horror. "Shall I tell you what triggered this?"

I nodded.

"My father used to take me hunting at night with his chums – to a place where children were not allowed. I had to hide under the seat as we went through the gate. They went to shoot buck – kudu, springbok, even eland. My Uncle Chas used to bring along a powerful spotlight and shine it into the bush as we drove. I'll never forget the feeling, the first time I killed an animal. I was the first to see her from the back of the truck, she was in a thicket. She was caught in the glare, as though paralysed by the light. She stared at us without moving, mesmerised. She was so beautiful, I forgot for a moment why we were there. I felt my father's body slide in behind me, guiding mine, his huge hands putting the rifle into mine and lining me up, helping me steady the rifle, setting the sights on that magnificent muscled shoulder, and helping me pull the trigger. She staggered at the impact, and tried to run, but couldn't. Blood ran from her shattered shoulder. My father took the rifle and chased after her and finished her off, with one shot to the head.

"It took four grown men to haul the animal into the back of the truck, right next to me. It was a kudu. I put my hand on her smooth hide, and stroked her belly all the way home, feeling the heat leave her body. I was fascinated by the gaping hole in her shoulder. I had to put my finger into the wound, had to feel how the bullet, my bullet, had entered her, flying through hide and muscle and bone as though it were paper. I felt the hard, sharp shards of broken bone, I smelt the sticky sweet smell of blood. The blood shone black on my hand in the moonlight. I felt ill, but also elated that I had the power to do this. I was only six."

Rory lit another cigarette, opened his mouth into an O like a fish and jerked his jaw, and watched the rings of smoke drift and widen on the air.

"After arriving home at our house in the bush," he continued, "we'd hang the beast up in a special enclosure and slit its throat, and gut it. My mother used to rush me off to bath and bed, but that night I made a fuss and got into trouble because I didn't want to wash the smell of the kudu, or her bright drying blood, off my hand. I couldn't sleep for thinking of her. That was when I heard my parents arguing deep into the night, and then came a crash so loud it made me sit up straight. A little later my mother came to my bed weeping, and climbed in beside me, and held me. I didn't know what was happening, or what I could do about it. In the morning there was a smear of blood on the pillow. I told myself it was from the kudu, even though I had bathed the night before. My parents never mentioned it, but from that night, I knew. I knew that somehow the kudu was me and I was her – we were inextricably linked."

He filled my glass, and smiled wryly at me, and said: "I don't know if any of that means anything to you. I mean, I'm against hunting now. Except for this," he said, turning to his latest canvas. "This is a kind of hunting. A kind of tracking down."

I looked at his work, and could suddenly see the kudu and the mother and the boy, all strung up and hung and bleeding. I felt less critical of the work, having heard the painful story of the small boy, but still, I would never hang it in my lounge.

Perhaps that should be enough for him, to feel whatever freedom he has conjured up by painting these scenes, these self-portraits. It is quite another matter to expose yourself to the glare of public scrutiny. It could result in his being shot down.

⌒

And I don't see what any of that has to do with Rory's argument about Jesus and bondage and freedom. I wish I were better with words, so that I could explain to him that he is mistaken. I wish to heaven that You would give me words, Lord, to further Your purpose.

You know perfectly well that if You don't, I keep saying the wrong things.

⌒

Dear God, dear God, dear God. Oh, Jesus. Blessed are the poor in spirit, for theirs is the Kingdom of Heaven. Blessed are the meek, for they shall possess the land. Blessed are they who mourn, for they shall be comforted. Blessed are they that hunger and thirst after justice, for they shall have their fill. Blessed are the merciful, for they shall obtain mercy. Blessed are the clean of heart, for they shall see God. Blessed are the peacemakers, for they shall be called the children of God. Blessed are they that suffer persecution for justice's sake, for theirs is the Kingdom of Heaven.

Words, strings of words to hang my prayers on, to pull me through.

What of those who serve, Lord? Will they also be blessed?

What of the trapped and the needy? What of the righteously angry? The confused and lonely? Will they be discarded? Forgive me for asking, but what of the overlooked, the second rate, and those tormented in the night? It is a bloody business, to hang on such a hook.

Stupid girl. It's all you're good for.

A river of shame runs through me.

Blessed are those who have given, for they will receive. Blessed are they who submit, for they will be exalted in Heaven. Blessed are the fearful, and those who have been hurt, those that despair, for they will be comforted.

Dear God. Dear God.

⌒

My chest struggles against the wintry night air as I sit and wait. Fear, and also the terrible damp, pull tightly across my chest, squeezing my air pipes, and I reach for my pump again.

It has occurred to me to sleep under the bed, but in order to suck in any air at all, I am forced to sit upright. I pray my chest will close, tight and forever. That is a way out of here. I think of the dead matron, how her lifeless body left through that door.

Today, terrified to be by myself, I went over to the art room. Suddenly I understand his paintings. This is what lies just beneath the surface. It is shocking to me, that I have never really seen that what I have been looking at all my life is a stupefying veneer. Just underneath lies this – viscous, raw, bleeding.

Rory asked me what was wrong, staring intently at my face as though one of his paintings lay reflected in it. I said I had the beginnings of a migraine, and the darling soul brought me an aspirin, and advised me to go and lie down. But I wanted to stay in the art room and not come back to this hateful green room. I feel safe there, surrounded by those visions of hell that have leapt from Rory's hand. I want to lie curled and covered up on the crude mat in Rory's office where he sleeps sometimes when he is working late.

In a moment of weakness I let a few tears escape, and he offered me his handkerchief, which was disgusting, but I was in such a state I blew my nose and wiped my face, and didn't care about the germs.

"You are very unhappy here," he observed, pouring me a sherry, even though I knew full well that sherry makes things worse.

If only he knew. I shook my head and tried to smile, which regretfully turned into a wail of grief. "I am sorry," I said, "I didn't mean to . . ."

He held me while I sobbed into his painting smock, its dried paint scratching my cheek.

"You are an angel," I said to him, trying to rectify matters with the aid of his handkerchief, concerned about the dishevelment I must present.

"I like you, Phyllis," he said. "You are a buried treasure." Which was a most unhelpful thing to say, as it set me off again.

Bury me deeper. Throw the stinking sods of life onto me until my mouth is stopped, and my heart finally breaks.

I sit and wait, putting every effort into breathing, minute by minute, deep into the night. I sit and watch the door.

⁓

I did not think the day would come that I would be grateful for my affliction, Lord! The condition of my chest saved me last night. When he arrived again, he found me in such a state, he took me straight to Groote Schuur Hospital, without even stopping to telephone Doctor Cudgel first. I could not speak, so little breath did I have left, but sat in the passenger seat, his wife's seat, and wondered how he would explain this to her.

I know this: once you lie about one thing, more and more lies heap on top of one another – all attempts to make the first lie more believable. It becomes easier, until you begin to believe your own lie – in fact, you cannot live without it.

My whole life has been one big lie, which is a sin before God, but I have not yet found a way to extricate myself. The whole damned edifice would then collapse.

He left me in the casualty section. I was sorry to be such a nuisance at that late hour, especially as there was a terrible commotion over at the non-white entrance as we drew up, with red lights flashing and ambulance personnel busy off-loading two stretchers. On the white side it was calmer, thank goodness. A nurse whipped a mask onto my face, and a kind doctor had a drip up in no time. Like a miracle, the clutching eased. Then, despite my embarrassment, I could not stop weeping. Now I am in the ward, writing on a piece of paper a nurse gave me, which I will stick into my journal. I pray I will find it safe on my return.

I do not want to go back. I want to stay here forever, with these dear nurses coming to minister to me each time I ring the bell. But only cowards run away. The boys are back today, and Michael is too, and I have abandoned my duties. I must return, for they need me.

It is not I who sin, is it, Lord? I didn't actually read *Lady Chatterley's Lover*. But it is true that I took it from Judy's hand, knowing full well what it was.

Perhaps it is possible to get used to someone sinning against you, if there is no other way. Perhaps one can be forgiven. I am certain many children have been bullied for the duration of their school lives, and have emerged blameless and intact in the sight of Our Lord.

Except that I will never graduate from this place. I will be like a pupil who perpetually fails her examination, and is doomed to sit out the last of her days repeating her fate.

You complain too much, Phyllis.

I will forget about it, and turn my mind to brighter things. There are many lives worse off than mine.

⌒

On one side is an Irish woman about my age, called Connie, who has a kidney condition. She used to be a tap dancer and has travelled the world. On the other is an older woman, Gwen, whose heart is giving in. She has blue lips and swollen ankles, yet regularly wheezes out of the ward wheeling her drip on a stand, in order to smoke a cigarette.

At visiting time Ursula arrived with George and a huge bunch of flowers. I don't know whether it was George or the flowers, but my chest tightened immediately and I was put on the mask again, so they could not stay long.

Then Judy arrived and brought me a book by an author I have never heard of, but I am afraid of Judy's books now. I think she has a streak that gets me into trouble. She does not walk with the Lord, and therefore lacks good judgment in certain matters. I will stick to the tried and trusted: Mr Dickens, and the Brontë sisters, and AJ Cronin.

There are books, I now realise, that should never have been written, however well intentioned the writer, and however well written they may be. Some subjects are inciting, and do nobody any good. I have heard that Mr Lawrence is a good writer, but there is good reason why the unfortunate book that fell into my hands was banned by the authorities. One simply cannot go about advocating sex outside marriage, and comparing the sex act to a mere conversation, or to drinking a cocktail. The likes of Mr Lawrence cannot accept that sex was created by the good Lord as a reward for getting married.

I had another chest X-ray today. It was deposited in the box at the foot of my bed, and so I took it out and had a look at it. Extraordinary thing, to see inside oneself. To think that that white blob is my heart, going quietly about its business. The good doctors say my heart is fine, but it is not. There is black blood in there, there is a tearing.

I am certain that an autopsy would reveal that my heart has become a ruined nest of scars.

⤚⟩

I must set this down, Lord, for it has been much on my mind. Worse than that, it has been keeping me up at night. My worries grind away like cogwheels, allowing me no rest.

How is it that the identical act can be so contradictory? Forgive me for speaking frankly, but surely the method You have devised for bringing Your children onto the earth, and which is also the expression of marital unity between man and woman, should not be so easily corrupted?

How is it that the same act can seem like an astonishing, tender gift, or be experienced as a terrible violence?

I sinned as a girl, but at the time it felt like the touch of love. A foolish part of me thinks that I can therefore judge the difference. The truth is, I have not heard from Alan again, not in forty years. The truth is that I have never experienced the act in the manner You intended – as sacrosanct and inviolable within a marriage. Oh, these tears! They will wash me away! The truth is that we are all able to deceive ourselves. This horror that is inflicted on me, *he* says he finds a comfort. Can each of us be so entirely alone in our experience of the very same act? Please help me, Lord, for I find myself in utter darkness.

⤚⟩

I have been remembered, which has set me off again, albeit quietly and into my pillow. I am afraid of drawing attention to myself and I am also concerned that Gwen in the next bed is dying. She no longer manages even to stagger outside for a cigarette. Her breathing has become a rattle, and the nurses have drawn the curtain around her and do things to her that result in a terrible sucking and gurgling, so things must be bad.

What makes me tearful at present – what it is to be the weaker sex! – is that Rory arrived last night at visiting time with a large envelope filled with get well cards that some of the scholars had drawn.

I like to think that they did not do this under duress. I like to think that one or two of them actually meant what they said. Michael's drawing of a horse was reasonably good. It is the first time I have seen his writing, which is very neat. He said he'd had a good holiday on the farm, where he rode horses, and he wished me a speedy re- covery. Dear boy.

Stephen Parsons drew me an excellent arum lily, and wrote me a limerick that made me laugh:

> There was a matron whose medicine
> Tasted like old boiled-up snakeskin.
> Be sure to get better
> When you get all these letters
> Or we'll make you take your own medicine.

And Adrian Flower drew a cup of steaming cocoa, which is what I give the boys when they stay over in the sick bay. Even Harry Slater made an effort. He drew a cartoon of a woman in a hospital bed with the doctor looking at her chart, saying: "I see that your results want to go home."

Rory is so kind, I don't understand why he bothers. What have I ever done for him?

This morning the professor arrived with some medical students and drew the curtain around my bed. He told the students a lot of things about my condition, but the only thing I remember is that asthma is an overreaction of the airways. That is certainly me! Always overreacting. Then the students took turns to listen to my chest, which was rather embarrassing, but I suppose it is in a good cause. There was one short young girl amongst them, with dull hair and an alarming bust, who smiled kindly at me and had the foresight to warm her stethoscope on her forearm before clamping it to my chest. I wondered about her, entering a man's world with all its complications. I saw she wore no ring. It is a good investment, education, if one does not have the looks for marriage.

The professor says I can go home tomorrow if I have a good night.

These cards from the boys have given me courage and hope. I will find a way through with Your help, Lord.

⌣

Gwen died last night. It was terrible to see her being wheeled off under a sheet. I am surprised, Lord, to find that I don't really want to die yet. The doctor told me that in fact I had almost died. I think that You were just trying to give me a fright.

To encourage me, You sent Michael after I arrived back at the school.

To my surprise and pleasure, he gave me a little hug, and said he was glad I was better. He was overflowing with the news that he has been chosen for a main part in the musical *The Prince and the Pauper* which the new drama teacher, Mr Collier, is putting on at the end of term. He is to be the Pauper turned Prince, switched at birth. I am so proud of him, and pray this will assist his popularity and integration in the school. Also, because it is the rugby season, he will not have to face the cricket team for a while.

He tells me his mother is well after her procedure, and will come down to see the play with her new fiancé, whom he has not yet met. Strange, how I guessed there might be another reason she did not have him home for the holidays. Poor child. I pray this man will be a good role model.

"Bring your mother to see me," I offered lightly, repressing the impulse to beg. "I'll make a chocolate cake for the occasion." Before he left, I took courage and held him to my bosom, and whispered in his ear that he is the best boy in the school, and he should never forget it. I believe there was a spring in his step as he went down the corridor. I believe that my prayers are being answered.

A bunch of giant proteas awaited me on my return. I do not know who put them there. I have always loved these strange and bulky blooms, simultaneously soft and hard. But my heart is damaged, and I cannot love these flowers for fear of who may have placed them on my bedside table, and I cannot remove them for fear that they may be seen to have been moved by the person who'd put them there. I am terrified of all repercussions, and move in small, slow ways, glancing about me. But at night I relegate the blooms to the bathroom, where their corpulent shapes wait alone until the morning light.

~

I don't know why I did it. I have shown Rory my paintings and draw-
ings. I never meant to, but he has been so kind.

He says they have merit.

He is only saying that, of course.

Yet there is a part of me that is bursting with pleasure, as though it
may be true. If only Phoebe could have heard him!

He especially liked the paintings of the mountain that are somewhat
strange and ominous looking, and those of the nest I'd found, where
my repeated efforts eventually resulted in a focus on its dark and
spoilt centre. He is astonished that I have never had an art lesson in
my life, and called me "a natural"!

I don't know what to do with this feeling in my chest, so light and
delighted that I want to skip!

Easily flattered, I am. Would he say what he honestly thinks?

These feelings are mere clutchings at straws.

~

From my room I can hear them practising. If I stop at the hall door, I
can watch them, these earnest and beautiful young men, my Michael
amongst them, transforming themselves into royalty and paupers,
working together with Mr Collier to transport us into the dilemmas
of the inequities of life, and how they might be resolved.

A few young girls from the sister school have been imported to
play the female roles. The one that plays Michael's mother has an

astonishing voice for her age.

> He's kind, he's gentle, he's things you'll never be.
> He thinks, he feels things, like trust and sympathy.
> He's not like you, John, a beggar and a thief,
> And that is why I love him so, this boy of mine.

The girl who is the love interest of the prince is better endowed physically, but her voice does not carry to the back of the hall. She has obviously been given the part for her sylph-like looks.

All these boys are princes; one wonders what they make of the story. In this country, to be poor is to be non-white, and an accidental swapping at birth would be impossible. But it makes one wonder – if it had been possible for a Samuel to have been exchanged for a Mr Talbot, for example, might Samuel have become Mr Talbot? Or would he have retained something of what makes him the Samuel he is today? Would he only ever have been fit for gardening work? And would Elizabeth, as the housemaster's wife, have had the boys doing African dancing before prep?

I am being ignored again both at table and elsewhere, which is a relief, but I do worry that it is some kind of calm before a huge storm. Please, Lord, send Your angels to protect me.

I am not sleeping well, despite the new medication which has done its job and opened my chest. Now that my passages are unclogged, I have noticed that my room still smells of death.

He came into the procedure room yesterday afternoon on some pretext – to ask about Gordon Wilcox's injury – and slipped a hand onto my breast. I immediately began to wheeze. It is true that distress goes to my chest, but in this instance I was putting it on. And it worked! He muttered something about being needed in the common room, and left in a hurry.

My chest, ironically, is the very thing that might save me.

Rory is painting the sets for the play together with some of the standard nines. He has asked me to join them. Imagine! I haven't even the clothes for it. They have set aside a corner of the art room for the huge panels, and they make a terrible mess. As an art teacher and a man, Rory can get away with looking dishevelled and paint-splotched, but in my case, this would be most inappropriate.

He just laughs at me when I point this out, saying he is certain that God got covered in mud while creating the beauty of the earth, and I should stop behaving like a princess.

I felt quite upset all afternoon. I have *never* been a princess! That role was inhabited entirely by Phoebe.

She wrote to say she will be down next week to look for a house, and doesn't know whether it is worth the effort of coming to visit me after my rude behaviour last time. She has a nerve! She should heed the advice of Jesus, who taught that one should rather attend to the beam in one's own eye.

Elizabeth is singing as she works, which previously may have irritated me; yet she has a voice, and a convivial spirit that is infectious.

She is far easier to have around than Grace, but I do keep thinking about the latter with concern.

⟅

I doubt I shall be able to read this scrawl tomorrow – somehow, the sherry has got into it. I am afraid to look again at what I painted to-night in the art room, for I am certain it is a horrible mess. I intended to paint a young man, using a photograph from a folder of images Rory keeps as a resource for his pupils. I chose him as my subject because I found the expression in his eyes quite compelling. He was staring up-wards into the heavens with a kind of longing that I wished to capture.

Rory must shoulder some of the blame for encouraging me to at-tempt a portrait, something I have not done in years. And he restrict-ed me to a blue palette, which has its challenges. Of course, it turned out all wrong. The poor fellow's features came out too feminine, and I was disappointed by my efforts. Yet Rory became quite excited; he is, after all, an art teacher, and must know something about the sub-ject. He encouraged me to "experiment", as he put it, by using longer strokes of the brush. I resisted this suggestion when he first raised it a few weeks back. Again I tried to explain to him that timidness is in my nature, just as untidiness is in his. A capacity for bold strokes is not what the good Lord had in mind when He made me.

But Rory is a stubborn man, and does not give up easily. He told me Francis Bacon reported that painting is an accident, and that one of his greatest paintings started off as a monkey, became a bird alight-ing, and finally a carcass. Mr Bacon apparently maintains that the im-age transforms itself through the actual act of painting.

I doubt that any of this has much to do with me, as I have absolutely no desire to produce ugly work like Mr Bacon's. But after arguing with Rory as we drank a few glasses of sherry together, my limbs felt loose and free. To my surprise, when I stepped back to look, the figure before me had begun to emerge curiously as a woman. And rather than the longing I had intended, she appeared elegant and strangely satisfied, her hands folded and relaxed in her lap. Rory declared it a self-portrait, but that is patent nonsense.

I am concerned that no one else should see it, and I should have brought it up to my room. Now it is locked away in the art room overnight, and I will just have to accept that, and try to get some sleep.

It is almost midnight, yet I am wide awake and quite exhilarated by it all.

If Mummy could see me now! Tipsy, with blue paint on my hands. What a terrible, terrible scandal!

Perhaps it is true what Rory says – if I have recalled his words correctly – that accidents and error often enough yield treasures. I know he was referring to the domain of painting, but I cannot help thinking of Michael. The world would be a lesser place if that sweet boy were not in it.

~

Today Elizabeth arrived limping. She tells me that she and Samuel got up at four this morning and walked all the way to work from the location because of a bus boycott! Perhaps they have had word of the American bus debacle, and are following the example. I wouldn't put it past Rory to have told them.

The skin had come away in places on Elizabeth's feet, and areas were bleeding. I felt annoyed – this was so unnecessary, especially given the perfectly good bus that the government kindly provides – and I found myself saying so while preparing an iodine solution in a basin. She sat on the chair with her feet immersed in the purple liquid, and shook her head and clucked and sighed, and pulled at her handkerchief and blew her nose until I felt even more annoyed, and told her that she should not make her life more difficult than it already is, and how on earth was she going to get home, and she should have known that this would happen.

Suddenly she looked up at me, and her eyes were lit with anger. "We do not *want* to stay in the location," she said, thumping her thigh for emphasis. "Our family had a nice home in Cape Town, and we were forced to move. Your kind government forces us to stay in the location because they say we have diseases. But we are good enough to work in white children's schools and in white homes. They make us live far away, and then they charge a third of our wages for their old bus!" She shook her head again. "Eh-eh, Madam, this is not fair. We cannot say thank you for things that are so unfair."

I was shocked. A non-white had never talked back to me before, and certainly not in an authoritative tone of voice. I wanted to give her a ticking-off for her rudeness, but I was unable to find a retort in the scramble of my brain. Father always said that non-whites who boycott are an ungrateful bunch, but what if Elizabeth's assertion is true? If so, I would have to scold the government instead of her! I found myself silently drying her feet and bandaging them up. It struck me, as I was on my knees in front of her, that I had never been so close to a non-white before. Shaken, I made her a cup of tea, and sat with her, and I said I was sure Mr Jansen would take her and Samuel home at the end of the day.

It seems that we all have our crosses to bear.

We ended up having a good chat, and because she has been much on my mind, the subject of Grace came up. Elizabeth says that Grace has no husband! When I asked who the father of the child is, she did her usual thing of clucking and shaking her head, and said that only God knows.

What on earth does she mean by that? Has Grace been sinning with several men? Or does Elizabeth know about Richard?

The other day, while standing at the sick bay window, I saw Grace cross the yard. She is far gone, and has started to waddle. What secrets lie hidden in that belly, in that tired face?

I remember how extraordinary it felt to have another life move inside me, to feel my own body distorted by another little person as she stretched a leg, or struggled to turn in the confines of my womb. No child is evil, but what if a child is conceived out of wrongful motive? Unlike Jesus, the cross I bore was of my own doing, my own undoing, as it is with that little coloured girl.

I pray for Grace's child, that it may find a way through. I pray that Grace will keep it.

⤚

Mrs Talbot has invited the matrons in all the houses to a Tupperware party at her house after the rugby tomorrow, together with some of her friends. I don't know what's come over her. What is a Tupperware party? I am too embarrassed to ask, as clearly this is something one ought to know. Also, why am I invited? If it is a card game, I will only disgrace myself.

I shall have to go or it will appear a snub, which I can ill afford.

It is all very uncomfortable.

I have never before been inside the Talbots' house.

⤙

There were several smart cars pulled up around the Talbots' house this afternoon, which I must say I found intimidating. If it were not for Mrs Calitz coming down the path, I probably would have turned tail and fled. I noticed that she, too, had put on her best, and after she had complimented me on my shawl, and I had admired her shoes, we had the courage to ring the doorbell. But once inside, being introduced to Mrs Talbot's other guests, we both looked somewhat shabby.

What a spread! This party was in fact not a party at all, but more a demonstration for a new product called Tupperware. I have to admit that Tupperware is a most extraordinary invention. It will completely revolutionise the lives of housewives. The lady who had come to demonstrate its many uses kept us all entranced. Imagine, a product made entirely of a plastic which is hygienic, unbreakable, airtight and watertight, with a seal that keeps food fresh and prevents spills. And the products come in so many wonderful colours! They are expensive, mind you.

Phoebe will love them. They are every woman's dream.

I excused myself at some point to powder my nose. I don't like to use other people's bathrooms, but tea does tend to go to the bladder. The whole way down the passage there were framed portraits on the walls of the Talbot family, and the Talbot children, all grown now, and gone. Two girls, both pleasant looking, and a boy holding a trophy, standing on a winner's box. An athlete, like his father. Then, across from the bathroom door, was the bedroom. Mrs Talbot had omitted to close the door, and inside the room I could see two beds. Perhaps there is something in what he told me, that he has not had relations with his wife since the children left. It was a cold room. A shudder went through me, and I suddenly felt as though I had eaten too much, and wanted to be sick.

Other people's bathrooms are dreadful places. They reveal private things one should never know about. The hairbrushes and toothpaste. The tweezers and razors. The toilet bowls where they seat their private parts. I could not bear to think of Mr and Mrs Talbot's nakedness in that sparkling, neat room with its top-of-the-range washing machine and its sponges resting on the soap rack.

As I looked around, I caught my face in the mirror that he no doubt uses every morning for shaving. What a terrible thought, to have my face superimposed on his.

There was fortunately no sign of Mr Talbot, but it was tempting fate to stay too long, so I thanked Mrs Talbot and left as soon as it was polite to do so.

Poor woman. She spent a huge amount on several Tupperware items, exclaiming with delight, but that is not going to save her soul or even her marriage.

Forgive me, Lord, something has gripped me, and I am afraid because I do not know whether it is You or Satan.

He came to me again last night. I got a huge fright, for the first I knew of it there was someone moving at my bedside. I shot up and must have made some sound in my consternation, for he stepped back, bumping the table and upsetting what I discovered this morning was the salt cellar, which had crashed to the floor.

"I'm so sorry, Matron," I heard the shape whisper above my tight, racing heart. Dear boy! What relief drenched me! "I could not raise you, you were fast asleep."

"What is it?" I asked him, groping for matches. I did not switch on the light, which I thought too harsh for that time of night. Even by the soft, wavering candlelight, I could see the poor thing was upset.

It was his tummy again, and he was shivering in his thin pyjamas, so I told him to jump into my bed to keep warm while I made him some cocoa and found him a tablet. Although there was no one in the sick bay, it seemed sensible to put him in a warm bed.

While the kettle boiled, I sat beside him and stroked his hair, and asked him what the matter was. It turns out that his mother is no longer coming down to Cape Town for the play, but is flying to the Greek isles with the new man in her life.

Forgive me, Lord, but I took him into my arms, as I imagine You would have done. We all have need of comfort. I got into bed beside him and held his sobbing body against mine until it quietened, and kissed the frown from his brow.

Forgive me, Lord, I am very afraid. Something has torn open in me, and fear has flown out, like batwings into my face.

I am haemorrhaging happiness, and I am half dead with fear.

I feel as Pandora must have done the moment she opened the box.

⤙

I watch him whenever I can, and rehearsals for the play afford me many opportunities. He seems to like it when I appear at the back of the hall, and throws his lines out for my ears, revelling in an attentive audience. He is not a bad little actor, and I have told him so.

He says he wants to be a film star when he grows up, like James Dean. Which worries me a little. If I recall correctly, James Dean killed himself last year through reckless driving. A wild character, not one to emulate.

Fortunately, it is highly unlikely that a young man from the southern tip of Africa would make it into the spotlights. It will therefore be a passing phase, and then he will settle down to something sensible and financially secure, like teaching or banking.

I must say I am strangely pleased that, unlike his grandfather, he shows no great interest in animals.

⤙

Dear God, please don't judge me harshly. Did You not bring me here for Your specific purpose? Have I not always been an obedient servant? Do You think it is always easy to know what is the best course of action in any given moment, any circumstance? Your commandments do not cover all the eventualities of life, and even those ten You have given us need interpretation. For example, surely You would not condemn someone who killed another in self-defence? Or someone who stole a loaf of bread to prevent his child from starving?

I have seen Your hand in all that has transpired. Yet I am confused, even afraid. Have I sinned, or have I done Your bidding? Do You look kindly on me, or have I displeased You?

I want to know what it is to love.

At night I lie awake worrying, but the truth is, rather than a sin, it feels like a gift, and at this late stage of my life! It seems a compensation for all that has happened. No one I know can ever understand this. No one. But You know everything, You have seen into my heart. You know I have only meant well.

⌒

Sometimes in the night, when the world is quiet, and the long rows of boys in the dormitories lie sleeping, he comes to me. There is a moment when the door first opens that my heart races in my throat with fear, but then I know it is he, for there is no dour odour of authority – thus far, and thankfully, the other seems discouraged by the unpredictability of my chest and stays away. The cold moonlight or black night lies heavy on my counterpane as I wait for the click of the catch and the hinge's creak as he enters. These sounds send sudden currents through me, releasing my body from corseted misery. I want to weep as he slides in between the sheets to lie beside me. Dear Lord, I pray silently as his head finds my shoulder and my arms enfold him, dear God, thank You.

He shivers; I clasp him to the warmth of my body, knowing how he suffers. He has confided that Roger and his henchmen have started victimising him again.

"It's all right," I tell him as he weeps in my arms like a baby. "It's all right, my darling."

I wish I could do more for him. Sometimes he wants to come to me in the day, or he reaches for my bedside light at night, but I cannot allow it. What we have is life and light enough – life and hope, a light held out against the menacing night.

When he leaves – too soon, always too soon – I am ill with shame and horror, and vow not to allow this again.

If only I could tell someone, someone who might understand these small, but brave human passions. If only real hope could emerge from these illicit meetings.

I cannot have this, yet I do have it, for this moment, and against all odds, against all hope. I ramble on now, an ageing woman. Yet I feel like the young girl I once was, my life full and bright with prospects. It was not to be. I ruined my future because of these dreadful aspects of my character: I am both wanton and wilful. I deserve everything that has happened to me.

Again I attract humiliation, annihilation. There will come a day when I am found out.

Tomorrow I will tell him not to come again.

⌒

I have seen the way he looks at her – the girl who plays his mother. She is about the same age as he, but no one else has noticed her much because of her homely looks and uneven teeth. I don't know what he sees in her, yet I have noticed them sitting together and talking during rehearsal breaks. He makes her laugh, all those terrible teeth sticking out as she throws her head back with unladylike hilarity. He tells me her name is Doris, and that she is a dancer as well as a singer, and that she holds a scholarship at her school.

I intercepted her after rehearsals this evening as she was coming out of the girls' cloakroom. "Doris," I said, startling her. She probably has no idea who I am. "I have seen how you flirt with the boys here. This is a respectable school, and we will not abide any unbecoming behaviour in young girls."

She had the grace to turn a bright beetroot, a sure sign of guilt. "Keep to the script," I advised her. "And keep your eyes down. You do not want to develop a reputation." She opened her mouth to say something, but stuttered and gave up. "Run along now," I said. "This is a serious production." She nodded and fled.

Anyone can see that she is not right for him.

Elizabeth arrived a moment ago with the news that the bus boycott is over, and the government has decided against the price hike after massive losses in revenue. Mr Jansen has been ferrying the African staff to and from the location for the past three weeks.

She is delighted, but in the end, has anything fundamentally changed? I fear we are all going under.

Looking into my face, Elizabeth asked me what was wrong. I could not tell her. Malaise comes to mind. Malaise, malady, malevolence.

Today her buoyancy is really annoying me.

I watched the play four times in all. First the dress rehearsal, then all three performances. It was a very professional show, despite the fact that Donald Gunn's voice started to break during his solo on the third night; also, during a particularly tense moment in the last performance, a piece of the set fell down. Michael soared in his role. He has a wonderful voice, strong and true. But it was clear that he sang for her. He knew that I was in my usual spot at the back of the hall where I would not be noticed by too many people, but he did not look once in my direction.

Yet I have been true to him, unlike his mother. I am the one who has stood by him and encouraged him. I am the one who has believed in him.

Mr Collier has arranged a small celebration, and as I write, they are all enjoying themselves in the common room. I was pleased to note that Doris went home immediately after the show. Rory and the boys who painted the sets have also been invited, but I, as usual, am left out.

Someone should tell that pathetic lion that it is pointless going on and on. Someone should put the poor beast out of his misery.

⌁

The holidays loom, and with them, loneliness. Michael's mother is back, so he is going home to her. She is no good for him. If only I could have him stay here with me!

You are not to forget me, I tell him. Some silly girl is going to snap you up one of these days, and then you will never come and visit me again.

He just laughs at me, and eats another biscuit. I tighten my grip on him, wanting to hold him to me forever, but he struggles free. In the candlelight, I watch him pull on his pyjamas.

"My chest has been so much better since you became my boy," I tell him. "Come and give me a last cuddle."

But he only gives me an impish grin. "Bye, Matron," he says, taking another biscuit.

I am left alone with crumbs between the sheets. He is a beautiful butterfly I cannot pin down, however much I try.

I saw a wonderful design for a cross-stitch in Mr Mandelstein's shop, and on impulse bought it as well as some embroidery cotton, which cost me a pretty penny. In a beautiful script, within an attractive butterfly border, are the words:

> *Yea, though I walk through the Valley of the Shadow of Death,*
> *I will fear no Evil; for Thou art with me.*

I will stitch it for him in the holidays, sewing each butterfly carefully into the fabric. It is my gift to this precious boy. It is my penance.

One day, when he is grown and I am dead, by this good thing he will remember me.

⌒

You stupid girl. You are doing it again.

I construct by my own hand the very thing that can be used against me. Once again, I carefully accrue evidence that could ruin my life. I should burn this, for I would rather die than have it fall into some-

172

one else's hand. Having reread certain alarming passages, I must attempt to explain to myself this contrariness of character.

The good Lord has deigned that we must live chronologically, and so our lives follow a storyline with a linear plot. But what if one could dip casually into the current of a life, or flip randomly through the pages of the days? How would it read then? How would the emphasis, the empathy, change?

If we could glimpse events simultaneously, at the beginning and near the end, would this help us to understand how a life has been shaped?

Would I then be forgiven?

Every day I reprimand myself, every day I consider burning this confession that merely invites shame and disgrace.

Human beings were not made to be alone. He is gone. He left two days ago with the other long-distance boarders. I walked down to the station with them in a light drizzle, both of us pretending in the straggle of schoolboys that we are nothing to each other. As the train accelerated out of the station, I waved at the heads sticking out of the carriage windows. His head was the first to disappear inside.

The first winter storms have struck, and I am continually cold. The holiday stretches before me like an inhospitable piece of coastline. Friends cannot be relied on, for they have their own pursuits.

What really upsets me is that Rory had said nothing to me about her.

This evening I saw slots of light through the shutters in the art room. I dressed up warmly and went over with a flask of coffee, full of the news that a pair of eagle owls is roosting in the palms near the hall. Imagine my shock on opening the door to be confronted by a naked woman hanging from the rafters! I suspect I let out a shriek as I stood there, paralysed, a hand over my mouth, not knowing what to do to assist her. Rory stepped out from behind a canvas, paintbrush in hand, as the woman lifted her head and shrieked too – though with laughter; her full breasts shook most horrifyingly with mirth. I then saw that she was suspended by a sort of makeshift harness about her chest. Below her, warmth radiated from a large heater.

"Phyllis!" Rory grinned, gesticulating ostentatiously. "Meet Griselda!"

Griselda! What kind of a name is that! The suspended strumpet held her hand out – or rather, down – to me. Her triangle of black hair stared me insultingly in the face.

I turned and departed, my cheeks stinging with rage and humiliation. How dare he! He will go to any lengths to make a fool of me.

He did not come after me.

As I sit on my bed I can see that the lights are still on in the art room, and it is already past midnight. What are they doing? Certainly they are laughing together about the frumpy little matron. I cannot bear to think of him looking at her naked body, let alone touching it.

I have lost a haven. I have been displaced. I am dispensable, after all.

I have no one to hold in the night.

⌒

Rory came knocking at my door late this morning. I suspected it might be him, though it equally could have been the other; either way, I pretended I wasn't there. He then resorted to making strangled little sounds outside until I opened the door for fear the noise might attract the attention of Mrs Williams or Mr Jansen.

He beamed at me through stubble, thinking he could charm his way out of the whole thing. "Come and see," he said, offering a hand streaked with paint.

"I am busy," I said.

"Please!" he implored with his boyish manipulations. I ignored the hand, but reluctantly followed him along the corridors to the art room.

He has painted her hanging from an abattoir hook, flayed, her skin stripped from her limbs. This is no nude in the tradition of the Great Masters, it is a travesty. She looks like a victim of torture, or a sacrificial offering, or a member of a cannibalistic culture. There are blue numbers in the background, blurred and receding; one does not know whether they represent criminal or mortuary numbers, or price tags, or butchery stamps on sides of meat. It is a terrible painting, nauseating.

Rory is very pleased with it.

"Who is she?" I wanted to know.

"My mother," he said. I stared at him, shocked. She is far too young to be his mother; then I realised he was laughing at me. What has happened? This man who has shown me such kindness has suddenly and for no apparent reason begun to mock me. Have I been mistaken about his friendship all along?

"So your mother's name is Griselda," I said stonily.

"Oh, no! Griselda is a friend."

"I have known you for a year, yet I have never met this woman," I said, realising that, of all Rory's friends, I had only ever met Pierre. I must be a terrible embarrassment to him.

"She has been overseas," was his excuse. "She's been studying in America for the past two years."

Do you sin with her? I wanted to blurt out. Does she like to be impaled?

"What is the matter?" Rory wanted to know.

"Nothing," I said. Absolutely nothing.

It can't be legal to have naked women in a boys' boarding school, even if it is the holidays. I have a good mind to report him.

⟅

The more I think about it, the more I see how Rory undermines the things that are right and good in the world. As I sat in chapel on Sunday, trying to concentrate on Father Nichols's sermon about Your terrible betrayal and death on the cross, my mind kept returning with a perverse obstinacy to the sight of that woman hanging from the rafters. It borders on the blasphemous, and Rory is intelligent enough to know it. Which all goes to show that it is not intelligence that will save us. The devil knows how to worm his way into the brightest of minds in order to subvert them.

Lord, please cleanse my mind and heart. Let me be worthy of Your great sacrifice.

⟅

Phoebe might know what to do. What a shocking thing! Elizabeth tells me that she and Samuel were stopped at the bus station by a policeman, who asked them to produce their passes. Samuel duly did so, but Elizabeth has not yet acquired one, as the new legislation requiring African women to carry passes has only just been promulgated. When the policeman found out that Elizabeth is married to Samuel, he told her that a pass would still not allow her to work in Cape Town. They don't want Bantu people in the Cape, she reported, shaking her head. The policeman said that the coloured people, who were here first, were complaining that the Bantu are taking their jobs, so the government has to be fair. If her husband has work, he might be allowed to stay, but Elizabeth would have to go home. He has given her until the end of the month, when she must go and live with her mother-in-law in the eastern Cape.

Samuel's family occupies a small piece of ground there, but there are no jobs in the area.

Elizabeth's eyes were wide with fury. "Your government chases the black people out of Cape Town to Ndabeni, then again to Langa, and now far away to the eastern Cape. What will they do to us next?" she clucked. "You want us to go and live in the sea?"

That wasn't exactly fair, I thought. I have never voted in my life. It is true, though, that my parents were National Party supporters, but that doesn't make it my fault.

"They want the married women to go," she fretted. "They want to break up our families."

"We'll speak to Mr Talbot," I suggested. "You have a good job here. They will persuade the authorities."

Elizabeth flashed her eyes at me. "I've already been to his office," she retorted. "He says his hands are tied. I said, 'Well then, untie them!' He just shook his head, and told me what Jesus said: 'Give unto Caesar what is Caesar's, and unto God what is God's'! I asked him who this Caesar is. 'It is the government,' he said. 'The law is the law.'

"White people made this law, Madam," she continued. "Why must black people obey it?"

I could not answer her. I must say, on reflection, I am embarrassed by my kind. She wept loudly, and I made her another cup of tea, but there is only so much comfort tea can give, and I ended up taking her into my arms, with her smoky smell and everything, and let her cry her black tears into my bosom.

I assured her that my sister would know what to do – that she'd be arriving tomorrow. These Black Sash types had better have more to offer than just standing around getting varicose veins outside Parliament.

⌐

The advice office is situated in Sybrand Park, a suburb near the location. When we arrived in Bryan's Mercedes at about nine in the morning, there was already a queue of Africans coming out of the door and onto the veranda. We had to step over the legs of people sitting in the passageway waiting their turn, before getting to the young African at a reception desk who was taking particulars and drawing up folders. Phoebe explained why we were there, and he gestured towards an adjacent room, explaining that there were two lawyers who were working as fast as they could, and that Elizabeth and Samuel would have to wait their turn. He started to help them fill in a form.

It was remarkable. Through the open door, I saw two smart young women behind desks, working through interpreters; one was listening intently to an elderly African whose face seemed to be carved out of sadness, and the other was giving audience to an angry, gesticulating African girl with a baby on her back. They were asking these Africans questions, and writing things down. It came to me with a tremendous shock that these young women were the lawyers!

The large, gracious house in a white suburb was full of Africans waiting patiently for assistance, full of their smell and their dirty children running around, and their loud conversation strung musically, pegged with clicks. I had never before seen so many of them all together in one place, and might have been frightened if I had not understood the situation.

These white women were working there all on their own, without a man to help or protect them. Trying to help this flood of people. Unafraid of drowning.

We left Elizabeth and Samuel there, and Phoebe took me out for tea. She was going on about the demonstrations that are taking place all over the country – African girls protesting against the introduction of passes for females. These girls were signing petitions and gathering together to throw their passes onto bonfires. In one village, when the mobile Reference Book Unit arrived to issue passes, they found only old men and children. The girls hid in caves nearby until they received the all clear.

I did not dare interject, but where does that leave Caesar?

Lord, how is a person to know when to accept one's lot on earth – which will always fall short of the perfection of heaven – and when to rise up and object?

Poor Elizabeth. We certainly could not just abandon her to her fate. She says that the family cannot survive on Samuel's wage. One of her sons is epileptic and cannot work, and she cares for two of her grandchildren whose mother died in a fire.

Phoebe slashed away at a piece of toast with her knife, and said that she cannot bear for her granddaughter to grow up in such a country. She declared that if the government continues on their course, there will eventually be bloodshed. When I objected, saying that even Christ had not raised his hand against his enemies, her eyes blazed. She said that if she were an African living in this country, she would be so angry she would kill.

What a terrible thing to say! I don't know where she gets her politics from. Our parents would turn in their graves to hear such a thing uttered by their favourite daughter!

Thank goodness, Lord, that in Your wisdom, You did not make Phoebe an African.

⌒

Rory has invited me to tea at Rhodes Memorial Tea Room this afternoon. With Griselda. He said with a smirk that she wants to meet me properly, with her clothes on. I can see that he feels sorry for me, a poor lonely old woman.

I told him I wouldn't dream of getting in the way.

"You won't be in the way!" he exclaimed.

I will. I have been. I always am.

I can make out Rhodes Memorial from my window, situated amongst green trees, with its statue of Rhodes proudly looking north to his great vision for the continent. We all have our visions, but sometimes that's as far as they get. Shoddy paintings of what might have been, smeared on the insides of one's eyelids.

That's where the two of them are meeting, right now.

I cannot imagine what he sees in her, but there you are.

His voice is breaking, and he has begun to shave during the holidays. My Michael is becoming a man. Soon he will no longer need me.

He was back in my arms the first night of the new term, telling me how he went hiking with friends in the Drakensberg. He doesn't like his mother's fiancé, he says. He is worried she is making a mistake.

"Is he kind to you?" I asked.

He shook his head. "He is rotten," he said. "That's why I went away with my friends. I can't wait to be grown up."

I wanted to tell him that it doesn't get any easier. I wanted to say that being an adult is harder than being a child, because you can no longer fool yourself that it will get better when you are older.

Elizabeth says that she has been advised to divorce Samuel! The lawyer says it is the only way she might be allowed to stay in her present employment, and in Cape Town. Married women are deemed to have the financial support of their husbands, and deemed therefore not to need to work.

She is very upset. "What will God say?" she clucked. "To survive the white man's laws, I must go against God's laws!"

Indeed, it is a very strange situation. "God will forgive you, Elizabeth," I reassured her, feeling certain I could speak on Your behalf in this matter. "God wants you to be with your husband."

These things have been a welcome diversion, a reason to get up in the morning, a motivation to leave my horrid green room.

My brushes are dry, my paintings are leaves before the winter wind.

What is to become of us all?

Is life really only a test to sort those who will ascend to heaven from those who will go down?

I am at best a leaky vessel, awaiting a final storm.

⤳

"You have struck rock!" That is what a large crowd of African girls have proclaimed to the Prime Minister of the Union of South Africa, Mr JG Strijdom, no less. I don't know where they get the audacity!

> Now you have touched the women, Strijdom,
> You have struck a rock!
> You have dislodged a boulder!
> You will be crushed!

I know about this, not from the newspapers, but from Phoebe. She has heard it from members of the Black Sash who have contact with

African women belonging to an organisation called the Women's League of the African National Congress. According to Phoebe's sources, twenty thousand African women travelled from all over South Africa to march on the Union Buildings in Pretoria in order to present a petition to the Prime Minister. Apparently he refused to meet with them, so they left their petitions there: over one hundred thousand signatures protesting against the new legislation forcing African women to carry passes!

You have struck rock.

Lord, You have said that rock is the only true foundation for a home.

Imagine – if I were to say to the housemaster: You have struck rock! Or if I had said that to Father, or to Mummy: You have struck rock! Or if I could say it even at this late stage to Alan.

They would laugh at me.

Or lock me away.

These second-class girls who have been born into a life with no prospects have put me to shame. It has shaken me to the core.

⟜

There are times one realises too late that the words one has uttered should never have been spoken. Terrible words let loose that one wishes to unsay, to somehow suck back in so that life might continue as if they had never been said.

Everything is lost. Everything has been spoilt. I cannot get the sight of Michael in the bathroom out of my head.

I am such a fool! To think I went to find him late last night, after discovering, soon after he'd left my room, that he had left his wrist-watch on my bedside table. I hoped to surprise him in the dormitory – to give him the watch and perhaps even lay a hand upon his head to feel again the radiant warmth of his young skin. If he were already asleep, I thought I might slip the watch under his pillow. I only wanted to show him that I am mindful of him, and that I miss him when he is not with me.

But only Stephen was there, snoring lightly in his bed. The only other place I thought I might find Michael was the bathroom, so I went quietly, to surprise him. When I think of it now, shame all but disembowels me – how I crept up so carefully, not using my torch, going only by the moonlight that was quite bright enough, my excitement mounting at the prospect of seeing my darling again, and at the possibility of another brief embrace. I heard water running and, knowing it was he, I went through the bathroom door, at first not understanding what it was I saw: Michael at the washbasin, his pyjama bottom pulled down and his top tucked up under his chin, thereby exposing the pale flesh from his chest to the top of his thighs, his beautiful young body revealed.

He was leaning his nether parts over the basin so as to wash himself. He was standing there, meticulously removing any trace of me with soap and water.

For a moment he was not aware of my presence. Then his head jerked up and his eyes looked straight into my face, his pyjama top falling down like a sudden curtain, covering the body I have loved so deeply, so well.

I saw his eyes widen with shock. I heard him suck his breath in and saw him yank his pants up, as if he thought I was spying on him. I saw in his eyes a look of pure terror.

Terror and disgust. The boy is disgusted by me.

I could not help it. An enormous wave of rage gathered itself, and roared through my body. The pressure was unbearable. I wanted to smack him across the face. I wanted to see his nose run with blood. I wanted to shout at him. With enormous restraint I managed to keep my voice down low, so it came out like a terrible growl. "How dare you!" I said, my voice shaking. "*How dare you!*"

I believe I pointed towards his dormitory. I believe I told him to get back to his bed *immediately*. He averted his eyes and bolted, making certain to slip sideways past me to ensure that he did not brush against me, that not one hair was contaminated by contact with me. He practically ran from me down the corridor, and did not look back.

At once I was struck with regret. I wanted to follow him, to go to his bed and implore him to come to me, to explain that it was all a misunderstanding. For a moment I didn't care who might hear or see me, or what anyone else might think.

But of course, of course, I could not go. I stood there in the cold corridor, collapsed with grief.

Dirty. Wild stinking kaffir. That's what I am. Rotten to the core.

Lamb of God, who takes away the sins of the world, have mercy on me. Lamb of God, who takes away the sins of the world, grant me peace. Lamb of God, please, God, wash me clean. My Lord, my God, stitch me into something whole.

It will take everything I have, but I will finish this. Yea, though I walk through the Valley of Death. I am in such a state that I had to unpick Death three times, and now the black thread will not lie completely flat. I cannot bear to unpick it again for I must finish it soon, and I am not even halfway. It will surely put things right.

I will fear no evil, for Thou art with me.

⌒

I know very well that the mountain is still somewhere out there in the night, and will still be there tomorrow and forever, as You are, Lord, but what good is this knowledge?

He has not come to me for eight nights.

Last Monday, I was pleased to come across him working at a table in the library, and approached him, but I was rebuked by Mr Richardson for whispering in the library. So I went outside and waited for him. When, after half an hour, he had not emerged, I popped my head round the door to find that he had disappeared. He could only have left via the fire escape.

On Tuesday afternoon, unable to concentrate on my duties, I sent word via Stephen Parsons for Michael to come to the sick bay. But when he came, he brought Stephen with him. I had to pretend that I needed to know whether he had run out of his asthma medicines. He shook his head, and they left. I was in such a consternation of disappointment that I forgot to offer them tea.

Then at break yesterday, outside the chapel, I managed to corner him briefly alone and told him to come to me tonight, but although he nodded, he has not come.

What has happened? Have his feelings really curdled into disgust? Dear God, have we been found out? Or has he met some Doris-girl?

Dear Lord, does every apparent gift conceal a punishment? Am I Your plaything, that You repeatedly give me something precious, only to take it away?

It is a quarter past three, and I cannot sleep. If he chose to look out of the north-wing dormitory window, he would see that my room is still lit by candlelight. He would know that I wait for him.

He does not like you, Phyllis. Like Alan, he was only experimenting.

~

It is nearly finished. Each stitch aligns the thread perfectly. As I stitch, the rhythm soothes me. There is a pattern here which pulls me through, which releases itself from the weave, from the seemingly random sequence of colour. These butterflies emerge from the chrysalis of the imagination.

This is for you, my boy. May it help you when I am gone.

~

This morning, coming into breakfast, I tripped on the threshold and fell to my hands and knees in front of the whole house. My burning ears heard a titter go round the hall.

Mr Talbot came to help me up, commanding the boys to be quiet. As I clambered awkwardly to my feet, pulling my skirt down, my knees grazed and aching, I looked up. With a terrifyingly clear focus, I saw, as if through the lens of a camera, that Michael, stationed behind his chair and next to Harry Slater, was one of those who had laughed.

~

Fifteen days, and still he avoids me. Why is this? What have I done?

Nowadays he sits with Harry Slater at break. That boy has no doubt revealed my dreadful nicknames, and has told my darling that I'd once sent him for a caning. I watch them through my window – these two young men who have not yet succeeded or failed in any significant way. They are pulling faces and punching each other's arms. They are rocking with laughter at some secret joke.

They are laughing, no doubt, at me.

He is drifting away. All I can do is hold him tenderly in my sight, and look at him across the terrible divide of wealth and age.

It is unbearable, yet I must bear it.

Above the bench where my Michael sits, and also contained within the frame of the sash window, I see the university on the mountain, presiding. Above that is Devil's Peak where, after the recent heavy rains, ribbons of water glisten in the morning light. And above that is You, Lord.

Everything I want lies tantalisingly before me. Everything I have ever desired is out of my reach.

~

He hates it. Although he thanked me, there was a moment, when he opened the wrapping, that I saw inside his face – a moment of utter horror – before he was able to compose his features.

It is, after all, an old rag with lifeless butterflies. How could I have thought to touch him with my pathetic effort?

⤺

His voice has not changed in forty years. Still mellow, almost musical.

"Professor Harris," he said. I could imagine him sitting in his important office, surrounded by important books. "Hello?"

I listened a moment to his breathing, then put the receiver down. I had already decided not to say anything. There is really nothing to say.

Oh, Alan! For so long, I actually believed that one day you would come and find me!

All I wanted was to hear your voice again, one last time.

⤺

It is over. Today I will give Mr Jansen some money, and ask him to go to the hardware shop. I am tired of waiting for keys that will never come. I am so very tired. I will ask Mr Jansen to install bolts inside my two bedroom doors.

Elizabeth has filed for divorce. God bless her. For her, there is another way through.

Today I will go to the bottom of the field and burn this journal. Fire is a good place to begin. These words will release themselves, blackened, into swirls of ash; they will mix and scatter on the winter wind. Only God will be able to decipher my story.

Tomorrow I will fetch my month's supply of medication from

Groote Schuur Hospital. Sixty tablets should be enough. I wonder how long it will take. I only pray I don't make a hash of this too, Lord.

Into Thy hands I commend my spirit. Please, God, You know how I always try to make the very best of things.

I always do.

DAWN GARISCH is a novelist and poet. She has also had a short play and a short film produced, and has written for the newspaper and for television. *Once, Two Islands*, her first novel for adults, was published by Myrmidon in 2008. She is a practising medical doctor, has two grown sons and lives in Cape Town.

Acknowledgments

Heartfelt thanks to John Cartwright, Veronica Cecil, Mallory Attwell, Katherine Glenday and Jenne Irving for comments on the initial drafts of the manuscript.

Nick Duffell's excellent publication, *The Making of Them: The British Attitude to Children and the Boarding School System*, published by Lone Arrow Press in 2000, assisted my insight into the psychological effects of boarding school.

I gleaned information about the origins of the Black Sash from the DVD *The Early Years* by DOXA Productions.